THE
TROUBLE
WITH
CASS

A Civil War Era Murder Mystery

C. B. HUESING

The Trouble with Cass
By C. B. Huesing

Copyright © 2012 C. B. Huesing
All rights reserved.

ISBN: 1480009325
ISBN-13: 9781480009325

Printed in the United States of America by CreateSpace.

THIS BOOK IS DEDICATED TO THE MORE THAN

SIX HUNDRED THOUSAND MEN, UNION AND

CONFEDERATE, WHO DIED IN THE

AMERICAN CIVIL WAR

ACKNOWLEDGEMENTS

I appreciate the editing and review assistance provided by Richard Beemer and Nancy Huesing, and the research assistance of Carol Macklin. Any errors or omissions are, of course, my responsibility.

C. B. Huesing

CHAPTER 1

CASS AND THE CIVIL WAR

It would be a short war according to the Northern press. The rebellion of the Southern states would be quashed in ninety days or less. "How dare they fire on Fort Sumter!" read the newspapers. In New York's Union Square, one hundred thousand New Yorkers gathered to demand vengeance.

Skirmishes became larger probing expeditions, and then came huge, bloody battles with enormous carnage. Kitchen talk around the country included new names like Bull Run, Shiloh, and Stonewall Jackson. The casualty lists grew longer and longer as the months wore on. The enormity of what was really happening was soon realized in every corner of our growing country, including the small town of Libertyville in central Indiana.

While her mother prepared supper, Cass Brooks sat at the kitchen table and read aloud the war news from the Libertyville weekly newspaper and then read the names of local men who were listed as casualties. She suddenly rose from the table and excused herself. "Mother, I'm going out front."

"It's getting chilly, Cass," her mother remarked.

Cass stood on the front porch, looking south and was lost in thought, thinking about the many men she knew on the casualty list. She wrapped her shawl more tightly around her shoulders as the fall air grew colder.

Almost all of the good men are off to war, she thought, *including my Matt. Let's see, he will be away for a year come Saturday.*

Cass was very worried, almost paranoid, about being a spinster. She had an aunt in Maine who never married. Aunt Edith visited the Brooks often; much too often for the Brooks' liking. As she aged, she became more bitter and cantankerous. *I just won't let that happen to me!* Then too, many of Cass' friends had already married, some as young as sixteen. It was 1862 and Cass had just turned nineteen.

Julie, Cass' younger sister by three years, stormed out of the house, slamming the door, startling Cass. "Well there you are, Cass! Supper's almost ready, no thanks to you," she said. She stopped and stood a distance from Cass with her arms crossed. "Land sakes, sister, all of your staring won't bring Matt home early. I fret about you and how you're behaving."

Cass turned, looked at her coldly. "Well, little sister, I have a handsome fiancé. You don't even have a real boyfriend. Maybe you should worry about finding a man like Matt! And, damn it, Julie, don't try to tell me how I should behave!"

Julie harrumphed and retreated back into the house. Cass turned and continued looking south. The corn had long been harvested, and there was nothing but brown, barren corn stalks as far as the eye could see. The cooler evening air met the warmer earth, creating a rolling ground fog which, like a shroud, began to cover the broken corn stalks. *Like fallen soldiers in a battlefield?* wondered Cass. *Oh Matt, please come home!*

Cass' long blond hair framed a handsome, almost masculine face. But her full lips, even nose, and wide, pale blue eyes softened the effect. She favored her mother, Martha, with her height and her patrician bearing. Her sometimes sharp tongue was, no doubt, a gift from her father, Ben.

Julie looked older and was wiser than her sixteen years. She was pretty, but plain looking compared with Cass. A head shorter than Cass, she took after her father's side of the family. She was big busted and broad beamed in the rear. Her hair style suggested the look of a schoolteacher, which she aspired to be. It was parted in the middle, smoothed back, braided, and pinned in a low bun at the back of the head.

Cass' parents, Ben and Martha, had moved from Maine to Indiana in 1840 as a young married couple at the urging of friends. Their friends wrote that "the soil was good, the land was cleared, and was available at a reasonable price." Martha's parents had given them a sizable wedding gift of money, and with part of it they bought a large parcel of land outside of Libertyville, about fifteen miles north of Indianapolis.

Ben was a carpenter and builder, a trade he learned from an uncle, and he built the first section of their home just in time for the birth of Cassandra. The two-storied house built of hewn lumber was nestled in a stand of grown trees, which sheltered the house from the cold winter winds from the north. "I don't like to farm that much, I'd rather build," Ben told Martha. So he left most of the farming of their acreage to tenant farmers, who generated income for them, and with the remainder of the money from Martha's parents, he started a building business. With good Indiana timber and limestone carted up from the quarries in southern Indiana, he became the favored builder in Libertyville County.

Over the years, as the county grew, there weren't many new buildings and homes that hadn't been built by Ben Brooks, including the Libertyville County Courthouse. He trained local men, along with hiring experienced carpenters and brick masons. Two of his best young men were Matt Johnson and Pleasant White. But Matt, his top foreman, was now off with the Union Army and Pleasant was bound to go if the war continued. Pleasant was the creative one. Ben built buildings that tended to look the same, but Pleasant designed and fabricated unique elevations and facades that enhanced their appearance.

With his success though, Ben became more profane and arrogant. He had little love for anyone outside of his family and was a tough taskmaster with his building crews. Most of his help hated him, and resented his endless cursing at them even more. But he paid good wages so they tolerated him. Local townspeople feared his ruthless ways of punishing people who got in his way. He was known for miles around for his wealth and power, and especially for his meddling in town and county politics.

Though short in stature, the barrel-chested Ben was stronger than most men, and was pleased when Cass told him that his crew called him "the bull" behind his back. He believed he earned this after several bare-knuckle fights when he first came to Libertyville, first behind his barn, as well as behind O'Donnell's Tavern in town.

Cass had so many of her father's undesirable characteristics that, two years earlier, her mother had sent her to Miss Adams' Finishing School in Fisherton, about five miles south of Libertyville. Martha had Julie join her. Cass was seventeen and Julie was fourteen. "You girls are privileged because your father has done so well in his businesses," their mother had reminded them. "You now have the responsibility to act like ladies and be good examples to the other girls in Libertyville. And I want an admired family; keep that in mind when you start thinking about men you might bring into our family."

Though it was only four days a month in the summer, Cass had hated both the buggy ride to Fisherton and Miss Adams' classes. They were held in her parlor near the front of her house which she kept closed except when she was teaching. Three other girls had been in the class, all gigglers when Miss Adams wasn't there. In a dry period, Cass could see dust rising from their chairs when the girls sat down, as if the cushions were giant powder puffs. If it had rained, the room smelled as musty as a just-opened, exhumed coffin.

All of this had been oblivious to Miss Adams, a portly woman about forty who wore a small bonnet, more like what the Amish women wore. The story reported by one of the gigglers had it that Miss Adams was "left standing at the altar in Massachusetts many years ago. She was so distraught that she moved to Indiana where there were friends, and started her life anew. At least that's what my mother heard."

She would come into the parlor, clucking and scurrying around like a chicken, counting noses, and then finally settling into her heavily-cushioned teaching chair with her book on her lap.

Miss Adams used *A Lady's Deportment* as her textbook. Each girl was required to have her own copy so that she could study it at home. The book covered all of the topics considered necessary to "refine" a girl in the 1860s: proper dressing, manners, introductions and salutations, etiquette in public places, courtship, and wedding etiquette. "Sit up straight in your seats, girls. Good posture is a mark of good breeding," Miss Adams would tell them. "Notice, please, that I called you 'girls' now. I will address you as 'ladies' on the last day of class, your graduation, if you do well."

Cass thought Miss Adams was pompous and boring when she would claim, much too often, that she was a direct descendant, a grandchild, of President John Adams. There was a portrait of President Adams hanging prominently over the fireplace mantle in the parlor. Miss Adams bore a striking resemblance to her homely grandfather. "Put one of Miss Adams' bonnets on him, and they would look like twins," one of the gigglers said when Miss Adams had excused herself. Hearing all the laughter, Miss Adams had hurried back into the parlor. "What is so funny?" she asked, frowning. No one volunteered to answer except Cass. "Well, we thought you and the President looked like twins."

Miss Adams didn't know how to take Cass' remark. "Well, we **are** closely related. Now back to our lessons."

"She worries about making us into ladies," Cass had said to Julie on the way home one day. "I worry about being an old maid like her. I think I would do away with myself."

"Oh, stop being so dramatic, Cass." Julie had said.

Cass and Julie survived Miss Adams' school, and matured a bit in the ensuing two years.

"Cass, I notice that you're not cussing as much lately," Julie said one day.

"Well, I've notice that you're not so much 'holier-than-thou,' little sister," Cass replied.

Cass now had a fiancé in the war, and Julie had a good friend who was a handsome young man. But what lay ahead for them was beyond the comprehension of the two teenage girls.

CHAPTER 2

MATT AND PLEASANT

Cass' thoughts often drifted to her fiancé, Matt. One day she told Julie, "I just can't wait for him to get back. He's the man for me. He's handsome, strong, and smart. Father said he was the best foreman he ever had. We'll get married as soon as he gets back and start a family. I want to be the grandest lady in Libertyville County. I bet Father will make us the richest couple, too." A chuckle and a rolling of eyes came from Julie.

Their mother felt the same about Matt. Martha had told her daughters privately that Matt was like the son they never had. "He even looks a lot like your father when he was Matt's age."

The last letter Cass received from Matt said that his regiment was moving fast, and that "he missed her a lot." Cass hoped in her heart that he would return a whole man and not be maimed. She had seen veterans returning to Libertyville who were severely disfigured, or were missing a limb, and she would cross the street to avoid looking at them.

Julie was not much interested in boys, but had a special fondness for Pleasant White. Like Pleasant, Julie had a talent for art using just pen and pencil. Often they met in the town park after Pleasant was done for the day at her father's office to show each other their latest sketches. Julie did landscapes and portraits, while Pleasant showed her his proposed building sketches. He also drew amusing caricatures of town locals. But more than anything though, she enjoyed walking with Pleasant along the banks of the White River. This closeness was despite her mother's objections; she thought Julie was too good for Pleasant.

Pleasant would tell Julie of his dream to study architecture as an apprentice in a prestigious firm in a large city. Julie would talk of her plans to become an elementary schoolteacher. One summer's evening, as the sun was setting, he held her hand as they walked along the river bank, then stopped and kissed her tenderly and said, "Julie, I love you." *What a wonderful man. I think I could marry this person some day!* Julie thought.

Olivia White told neighbors that she was glad she named her fourth son Pleasant because, "He was such a sweet baby who hardly ever cried. When he did cry, one of his brothers would run to his crib and soon have him content."

Pleasant grew straight and strong, and was soon with his brothers in the fields and animal pens, helping his father, David. Pleasant used his lanky yet strong frame to hold his own when wrestling with his older brothers and neighbor boys. Towheaded, blue-eyed, a shade over six feet tall with a strong chin and a genial innocence about him, he turned the heads of the girls in Libertyville. Pleasant didn't seem to notice this, as if he had other things on his mind.

The Libertyville County Fair committee heard that when Abe Lincoln was young, he could hold an axe horizontally with one arm longer than any man in his county. Consequently, the contest was introduced at the next county fair. Pleasant outdid a dozen competitors and won a fine, young pig for his family. He also won a little money on side bets made at the fair's horseshoe-pitching contest. He would first best a man throwing right-handed, and then, doubling the bet, he would beat him again pitching left-handed. He never lost a match at the fair that year.

Pleasant picked up the carpentry trade from his father, and soon was doing repair work around Libertyville. He did good work and made friends easily. "Pleasant, you could earn more money if you spent less time swapping tales with your customers," his mother would say. Pleasant still made time to study all of the building design books at the Libertyville library, and rode his horse to the Indianapolis library whenever he had a free day to peruse its architectural design books and to study new buildings.

His carpentry know-how soon caught the attention of Ben Brooks, who learned from Julie that Pleasant also had drawing skills. "Father, I bet Pleasant could sketch nice renderings of your new buildings you're planning," said Julie. After reviewing his sketches, Ben hired him for the office. Although he thought Pleasant was too laid-back for his liking, he had to admit that his design skills greatly enhanced the appearance of his buildings and residences.

According to the Provost Marshall's office, Pleasant was due to be called up in the next six months. His mother, Olivia, prayed that the war would be over by that time. Two of his older brothers, Joseph and Mike, were already gone, serving somewhere in West Virginia. Another brother, Tim, remained home since he was declared unfit for the army. He had been thrown from his horse, landing face-first on a large field stone, breaking off his front teeth. Four front teeth were necessary to tear open powder packets for firing; as a result Tim received a 4F designation. (Soldiers tore open the packet with their teeth, poured the powder down the barrel, dropped in a mini ball, and then rammed the works down the barrel with a rod.) His father, David, was sorry for Tim's injury, but was pleased that he would have at least one son home to help work the farm.

Pleasant didn't want to leave, but was confident he would return. He was a crack shot and hoped that this would help him survive. "Pleasant should go hunt some game," Olivia often said. His brothers would laugh at her obvious preference, but they knew they would likely eat rabbit, squirrel, or quail that night.

Pleasant's faithful companion was his dog, Shadow, a mixed breed that had a good amount of hunting dog in him. He never left Pleasant's side and walked beside him when he was plowing or feeding the livestock. Pleasant's mother named the dog Shadow. "Look for Pleasant and you'll find the dog, and vice-versa," Olivia would say.

David enjoyed sitting on his front porch after a hard day's work, puffing on his corncob pipe. Pleasant and Shadow would often join him. As they rocked away, they would talk about everything, but mostly about the war.

Pleasant said he didn't like the idea of shooting boys his age. "How did this thing start, Pa?"

"Pleasant, I'm just a farmer, didn't have much schoolin'. Did do numbers and reading lessons, that's about all. Can tell you what I heard from the barber shop and from sitting around on the benches in front of the courthouse on Sunday after church."

He took a few puffs on his pipe and continued as Pleasant listened. "When Lincoln and his Republicans wanted to end slavery, the southern slave states commenced to quit the Union. Lincoln didn't want a fight, but when the Confederates fired on Fort Sumter the fight was on. Most folks thought it would be over real soon but they were wrong. At Bull Run, the Confederates kept charging and routed the Yankees. They are a tough bunch who don't like Washington telling them what to do. Son, I know you don't like killin' anymore than I do, but you have to kill them or they will kill you. I hate to see you go, but I 'spect you will have to join your brothers."

Pleasant never backed down from a fight. "Pa, I'm no better than Joseph and Mike," he said. "I'll do my share."

As winter came, Pleasant thought of his good friend, Matt Johnson, wondering if he was in the middle of a fight with the Confederates. At that moment Matt was just east of Nashville, Tennessee, slinging his Enfield rifle on his shoulder and falling into ranks. Various elements of the Union army had rendezvoused there for an offensive engagement with the Confederates, who were reportedly encamped just south of Murphysboro, some sixteen miles away. Pleasant was very close to being right.

CHAPTER 3

THE BOYS ARE IN THE FIGHT

Matt Johnson was one of forty-three thousand Union soldiers under General William Rosecrans who marched from Nashville toward Murphysboro on December 26, 1862. Christmas was soon forgotten as the company commanders formed their men three abreast, and then merged their new, untried recruits with veteran troops into the main line when ordered. The column of men moved slowly so they wouldn't outpace the mules and oxen pulling the cannons and supply wagons. Matt was sandwiched between two men, who were plodding along with heavy backpacks.

"What's your name, fella, and where you from?" asked the man on his left.

"Matt Johnson, Libertyville, Indiana, just north of Indianapolis. How about you?"

"Caleb Walker. My old sergeant called me 'Talkie,' so you might as well call me that too. He traded me to this company 'cause he said he was tired of hearing me talk. I'm from Tall Tree, Indiana, about two days ride southwest from Indianapolis. There's a huge sycamore right in the middle of the town. Biggest tree you've ever seen! Don't know what we're gonna call the town if that tree ever falls down."

"My Ma says we live where the hills start rollin' south toward the Ohio River. Well, I talk a lot 'cause my Ma says if you don't get what their sayin', or don't know why things are the way they are, ask questions! So that's what I do."

He took off his cap and wiped his brow. Caleb was a rotund, short man, with early balding.

"Ma said I look like a monk, like my grandpa. He died early; didn't know him."

"Matt, do you know how these people get to be officers and ride horses while we walk?"

"I guess they are commissioned."

"Well, what's that mean?" asked Talkie.

"I think some men are put up by county officials, and the Governor commissions them as officers."

"I hear you, Matt, but I hear tell there's some bad stuff going on, like some rich guys pay to be an officer. Hear what I'm sayin'? "

"Never heard that, Talkie. That would be bad if it happens."

"Well it happens, Matt. Sure as hell happens!"

Matt thought he was through, but Talkie wasn't done yet.

"Yep, they ride their fancy horses up front with the flag bearers when we march through towns. You watch 'em. I hear tell that when the shooting starts, they skedaddle to the rear where they say they can see the whole field of battle better. Hogwash!"

Hearing all of this, one grizzled, older soldier up ahead had had enough. "Talkie, you sure make us feel good about the army and our officers. Have you been in any battles or skirmishes?"

"Well, no. Just hear tell."

"Well, I have, and our officers were on the front line and led our charges, so watch your mouth, kid!" He paused. "Tell you what; we're going to find a mule for you, and put you up front. You'll talk the Rebels to death!"

The soldiers who were near let out such a roaring laugh that their sergeant ran back to the noise, and collared Talkie. "I knew it was you again! Damn it, Talkie, didn't I tell you to shut the hell up? Confederate scouts can hear us from a mile away! Next time I'm pulling you out and putting you in the rear of our column. You'll be digging latrines every day for the rest of your enlistment. I never should have traded for you. You hear me, boy?"

"Yes, Sergeant."

Talkie just couldn't stop talking, so he bowed his head, kept walking, and continued in a muted, mumbled, soliloquy in which he cussed officers, governors, and sergeants.

To an eagle soaring high above, the long column of soldiers looked like a giant serpent slithering slowly through the forest. At its head were its flickering eyes created by the fluttering of colorful flags.

The Union force made camp four days later near the Stones River, about two hundred yards across the river from the encamped Confederates. Their respective army bands began competing with one another, playing southern and northern pieces. Then when one band played *Home Sweet Home*, the other joined in. Soon there were some eighty-one thousand men singing the same favorite song together in the cold night. The sound of singing could be heard on nearby farms by those who hadn't fled. They wondered what was happening. The strange, peaceful interlude would soon end when the battle began.

At dawn, the Confederates seized the advantage by striking first from across the river. Having been at winter encampment for weeks, they had time before the Yankees arrived to explore the best shallow places to cross. Fierce fighting began. "The boys are in the fight!" General Bragg yelled. The roar of cannon and musketry was deafening. Matt and his battalion were placed on the left flank, where they could send a heavy crossfire at the Confederates, who were formed up in ragged ranks: marching, stopping, kneeling, firing, reloading, and marching again. Matt managed to get off three rounds with his Enfield rifle, striking gray uniforms with two of his shots.

Suddenly, in a loud chorus, the rebels yelled, wheeled right, and charged toward Matt's battalion's position. The rebels' screaming yelps sounded like something between an injured dog's cry and a wolf-howl. They ran so fast in their charge that the Union troops couldn't reload fast enough to return fire. Within seconds they were fighting hand-to-hand, beating back the attack with bayonets and rifle butts. Matt pulled off his bayonet from his rifle and swung it by the barrel at the nearest rebel's head. The barrel was hot from firing but Matt didn't notice. The Confederates slowly retreated, stopping to reload and fire as they waded back across the river. Matt's uniform was spattered with blood. In a state of shock, he trembled as he stared down at the bodies littered around him. He couldn't tell if the blood on his uniform was his or theirs. He searched his body for wounds and decided it was theirs. It was his first taste of battle and he had survived. The dead Confederates were dragged to the rear and stacked up in rows like firewood. The wounded were taken captive and their wounds treated.

Matt looked down the line and saw Talkie being rolled on a stretcher with what looked like a wound to his leg. Of course, he was talking.

"Did you see those crazy Rebels charging? Am I hurt bad? I think I'm bleeding to death! Will I lose my leg? Where you takin' me?"

The next day, New Year's Day, was quiet except for occasional sniper shots from both sides. A hard rain during the night had turned the fields into a precarious quagmire. Both sides remained in position, binding their wounds while they planned their next move. Matt slowly cleaned his rifle under his tarp, his mind drifting back to Libertyville and Cass. *The folks back there have no idea how awful war can be,* he thought. *Well, maybe Cass is praying for me right now.*

Near dawn the next day, Matt was shaken awake by his platoon sergeant, Jeb Cotton. Matt's limbs were stiff and cold. To conceal exact positions, campfires were not lit for three nights. The silhouette of a soldier against firelight also made an easy target for a sniper. The sergeant motioned toward an area behind a breastwork fortification where they joined the rest of his squad. Cotton, in a hushed voice, said, "General Rosecrans has ordered us to charge across the river and send those rebs to hell. Companies C and D will join our Company on our left and right flank. Yep, we'll be on the point of this charge, but there will be a lot more of our boys crossing down river to get their attention and distract them."

Matt and his fellow troopers slid quietly down a muddy bank into the cold waters of Stones River. The water was knee high as they struggled for the other bank. A surprised Confederate sentry finally caught sight of them in the semi-darkness. He yelled and fired off a round, rousing the sleeping Confederate soldiers. They were quick to their guns and began to pick off the Union troops, who were now halfway across the river. It seemed to Matt that the other bank was a mile away. His heart thumped wildly as he saw the rising smoke and heard the muzzle blasts firing at them. Rifle in hand, he finally reached the other side and tried to climb up the soft, muddy bank, clawing with his free hand and digging his boots into the mud. Then there was sudden darkness as a mini ball struck his head. Other Union troops climbed up the bank, using the bodies of their fallen comrades as leverage. Reaching the top of the bank they were met by hails of grape shot from Confederate howitzers. Men fell by the scores. The troopers who were not hit slid down the bank into the river, putting them at the mercy of rifle fire once again.

General Rosecrans, riding back and forth on the Union side of the river, exhorted his men to hold. Rosecrans' aide, riding by his side, had his head blown off by a Confederate cannon ball. A shocked Rosecrans yelled for the bugler to sound retreat. A bugle call was not necessary; men were swimming and running for their lives. The hundreds of bodies floating in the blood-red river were turned slowly by the current and drifted downstream.

The survivors of the ill-fated charge regrouped in the safety of a ditch thirty yards from the river. Sergeant Cotton, holding a bloody cloth to his shoulder, took a roll call of his men. When he came to Matt Johnson, one soldier said, "I was right next to him on the bank and saw him take a shot to his head. Knocked his cap off. His blood hit me in the face. He be dead." More than half of Matt's Company had been killed or wounded.

The battle continued through the day with charges and counter-charges. Casualties mounted into the thousands on both sides. As dusk approached, the fighting slowly stopped as the weary men seemed to have had enough killing for one day.

A bright, warm sun greeted the armies the next day. By noon, the corpses from the first day of combat started to decay, emitting a sweet, sickening smell. General Bragg looked up and saw hawks and turkey buzzards circling the battlefield. *Coyotes and wild pigs are next in line for our bodies*, he thought. He ordered Confederate details to dig deep mass graves while the main force waited for another charge from the Union side.

"What about the dead Yankees?" asked a soldier.

"Throw them in with our boys; they ain't quarreling no more," a sergeant said. "They'll be sorted out later. But first take their boots, guns and ammo. Our boys can use 'em."

On the Union side, bodies were dragged quickly from the front lines to keep up the morale of the surviving soldiers. Federal details buried them in individual, shallow graves in nearby fields.

Early the next day, the Confederate army moved out slowly to the southeast, fighting in half-hearted skirmishes with Union troops on the way out. It was a fruitless battle at Stones River; nobody really won. Rosecrans proclaimed a Union victory after Bragg withdrew, but the battle cost thirteen thousand, two hundred forty nine Federal casualties and ten thousand, two hundred sixty-six Confederate. Bragg and Rosecrans would meet again in battle six months later at Chattanooga, but without Matt Johnson, a brave boy from Libertyville, Indiana.

CHAPTER 4

GRIEVING MATT

The Provost Marshall brought the news to James and Mary Johnson. They were in shock and disbelief. Their only child, Matt, strong, handsome, and beloved, was dead at age twenty. A letter from a Captain Browning read, "Matt Johnson was a brave young man who served his country well. We believe he is buried in one of the many mass graves dug by the Confederates along the Stones River during a battle near Murphysboro, Tennessee. His body will be recovered in due course. You will be advised at that time. Please accept our heartfelt sympathy for your loss."

Cass cried for two days, for her fiancé, Matt, and for herself. She wrapped herself in a heavy cloak and walked slowly in the January snow. *Now what do I do? I feel like a widow but I'm just an unmarried spinster.*

Cass thought about the best men left in Libertyville. Bill Draper was engaged to June Felger. Charlie Cox was marrying Susan Fry, so Pleasant White was the best of the rest. Cass knew her sister, Julie, really liked Pleasant, but he was fair game in Cass' mind.

It didn't take long for Cass to make a move on Pleasant. She started in her father's office by admiring his sketches of planned buildings, looking over his shoulder and caressing his neck. Next she asked him to sketch a picture of her. Pleasant obliged. As she posed for the picture on her front porch, she unashamedly charmed Pleasant. Julie could see what was going on but she knew she couldn't outdo Cass. She tried once to assert herself and confronted Cass. Cass looked at her, smiled sweetly, and said, "What on earth are you talking about?" Julie was angrier at Pleasant than she was at Cass. She couldn't understand why Pleasant was so easily seduced by Cass' deceiving ways. He had told Julie that he loved her, and now this. *How quickly my love has turned to bitterness. I hate that man,* she thought.

Pleasant was at first surprised and then elated that Cass wanted his company; she was the prettiest girl in Libertyville by all accounts. To Julie's chagrin, they began taking long walks together, holding hands and laughing. Then one evening, near the Brooks' house, Cass offered her lips to Pleasant as they said goodnight in the approaching darkness.

Julie resigned herself to her fate and began looking around town for a new beau. There was the son of the dry goods store owner, Sam Coates, who seemed nice and kind. He had a serious hearing problem that Julie understood would keep him out of the army. That was a good thing as far as Julie was concerned. And Sam would probably take over the store from his father some day. Julie started shopping at the dry goods store more often.

Things happen fast in time of war, and within a month a wedding date was set by Cass and Pleasant. Ben and Martha Brooks were not happy to have Pleasant in their family. They had wanted Matt Johnson for a son-in-law, not only because he was their favorite, but also because the Johnson family was fairly well-to-do; more in their class. Pleasant's family was a good but struggling farming family.

The wedding was held in the flower garden of the Brooks' home, and the elite of Libertyville County attended. They seemed to need a relief from all the sadness brought on by the war. Already more than a hundred Libertyville County men had died and twice that number were wounded. There was much dancing and drinking that day at the wedding.

Cass wore a beautiful, white satin dress. Her full skirt was held out by hooped petticoats and crinolines. A circlet of flowers adorned her hair. Pleasant looked elegant in a gray, three-piece suit with a sack cloth jacket, waist coat, and tailored trousers that Cass ordered for him. Cass looked regal next to her lanky husband. Julie was Cass' sober-faced bridesmaid and Jim Bartlett, Pleasant's boyhood friend, was his best man. Ben Brooks, the father of the bride, reluctantly handed his Cass to Pleasant.

The couple took a buggy to a guesthouse in the little town of Middlefork. Cass pretended innocence in the darkness of the spring night even though she had gained some experience in the arms of Matt before he left for battle. She led an awkward and cautious Pleasant gently but firmly, feigning pain at first. Alarmed, Pleasant stopped and said he was sorry. *Too much acting*, she thought, and took him back gently, murmuring softly this time. *At least I am married, no longer an old maid*, she thought as she awoke in the morning.

CHAPTER 5

ANOTHER SOLDIER

The newlyweds had hardly returned from their honeymoon when Pleasant was called for the army. They stayed in a wing at the Brooks' home since the house Ben was building for them nearby was far from being finished. The 30-day notice that Pleasant received went by quickly. Pleasant joined fifty other recruits at the Libertyville train station where they were sworn in by the Provost Marshall as relatives and friends stood nearby. Cass, Olivia, and David saw him off. Ben, Martha, and Julie were not there. As the men boarded the train, Olivia cried, but Cass couldn't bring up a tear for Pleasant. Neither did she tell Pleasant that she thought she was pregnant.

Arriving at Union Station in Indianapolis, the recruits were met by a Federal drill sergeant and were marched, out of step, to Camp Sullivan, about a half-mile away. Told to change their clothes, they were given Union blues with a cap, boots, underwear, a rubber blanket for the ground or rain, a woolen blanket, and a small shelter tent, along with other items for the field. Their civilian clothes were gathered up to be given to the poor. After a restless night on hard ground in their tents, they were rousted for another roll call, and given hot breakfasts. Rifles and ammunition were issued to each man, and marching, drilling, and practice-range firing went on for more than a month.

One admonition from the firing range instructor stuck in Pleasant's mind. "Many a new man gets excited in the heat of battle and forgets that he already loaded his rifle," he said. "They'll pour some more powder and another ball down the barrel and ram it home. Some boys are so nervous they'll do it more times. They pull the trigger and the rifle explodes in their face. So if you want your nose in the same place when you get back home, remember what I just said."

Pleasant's group was formed into a company that was merged into a regiment of four thousand men from other Indiana towns. Pleasant was selected to be a squad leader of twelve men because the drill sergeant decided he had leadership qualities; also he was a good shot, and was taller than most. The sergeant told Pleasant that taller men automatically commanded more respect, all other things being equal.

The young lions in his squad thought differently. One in particular, Henry Hughes, took the lead. He was almost as tall as Pleasant but heavier. "Hey Slim," he said. "You have battle experience? Is that why the sergeant made you a squad leader?"

"No," said Pleasant. "I don't know why he picked me. Why don't you go ask him?"

"Oh, a smart-ass kid, huh? Well, I think I'll give you some battle experience right now." He started rolling up his sleeves. "They call me 'Kokomo.' That's where I'm from. What's your name, Slim? I mean your real name?"

A small crowd of recruits had gathered by then.

"Pleasant White," he answered.

"Pleasant!" he roared. "Well, you got a pansy name for a squad leader! Let's see if the pansy has any fight in him."

Kokomo started with a round-house right cross, which Pleasant deflected with his left arm and countered with a straight fist to his face. Kokomo staggered backward and caught himself before falling.

"I think you broke my nose, you bastard!" He then ran at Pleasant full-bore, but Pleasant side-stepped him and threw him to the ground. Pleasant had wrestled his older, bigger brothers and the neighbor boys for years, and he soon had Kokomo in a scissor hold with his long legs crushing Kokomo's middle. His right arm was wrapped around his neck in a choke hold. Kokomo's arms slapped the ground and he finally gurgled "give" through the blood that was running from his nose into his mouth. Pleasant tried to help him up but Kokomo said, "Leave me alone."

No one else chose to challenge Pleasant. Kokomo got over his defeat and slowly became Pleasant's sidekick. "We're gonna run those Rebels home, ain't we, Pleasant? Hey, you can call me 'Henry.' You and me, we make a good team. We'll watch each other's backs, okay?"

"Are all the boys from Kokomo as tough and feisty as you?" Pleasant asked.

It was difficult for Henry to answer a subtle, rhetoric, question directly and quickly. He had to sort things out. It took him time to think and find words. He just stared at Pleasant.

"Well, I'd be mighty pleased to have you watch my back, Henry, and I'll watch yours."

The Indiana regiment was loaded on successive trains, which headed east through Ohio into Pennsylvania, finally arriving at Harrisburg. From there they marched southeast and bivouacked near Elizabethtown. Rumor had it that the Confederates under General Robert E. Lee had brazenly crossed into Pennsylvania from Maryland, but nobody seemed to know where. The regiment was ordered on the march again and was told they would soon join elements of a much larger force, General Meade's Army of the Potomac. Now Pleasant was soon to be part of a Federal force of eighty-five thousand men. *How can the Rebels stop a force like that?* he thought.

Lee's army of sixty-five thousand men moved slowly in the hot, July sun, feasting on ripened cherries as they marched into Pennsylvania. They would regret eating too many cherries as they went into battle. The whole force had slipped in undetected, using the west side of the Blue Mountain range as a shield. In the evening the massive force camped in and around the village of Cashtown, eight miles northwest of the town of Gettysburg, a road and rail hub in Pennsylvania.

Pleasant's regiment went southeast and managed to hook up with the cavalry unit of General John Buford, whose strategy was to secure the high ground around Gettysburg before the Confederates arrived in force. Buford had already stopped several probing Rebel attacks, but with a loss of many of his men. He was surprised and happy to have Pleasant's regiment reinforce his. Meade's main Union force was still a few hours away, coming up from the south.

The Federals fortified their defensive positions on Cemetery Hill and waited. One of Pleasant's squad members laughed as he read aloud a sign posted in front of the stone archway leading into Evergreen Cemetery. He read: *All Persons Found Using Firearms in These Grounds Will Be Prosecuted With the Upmost Rigor of the Law.* The Union troops slept uneasily on the cemetery ground in the warm Pennsylvania night. Some used flat grave markers for headrests. Pleasant thought of Cass and his mother and prayed before drifting off to sleep.

At dawn, General Ewell's Confederate troops moved in force down Cashtown Road toward Gettysburg. The faraway rumble of horse hoofs and wagons sounded like a storm front approaching. Reaching the outskirts of town, they spread out and advanced up Cemetery Hill and Culp's Hill. The Union cannons had not been moved up yet, so it was up to the riflemen to hold their positions. The gray lines of Confederates moved steadily up the hills. The company captain told Pleasant and his boys to "hold your fire until they are about two hundred yards away." Pleasant lay on his stomach behind heavy timbers with Henry next to him, and began firing on command. He aimed at their knees to compensate for the barrel jerking upward when fired. He could get off three rounds per minute with his muzzle-loading rifle. He dropped five of the charging rebels, and as he reached up to ram another load down the barrel, he was hit in the right arm with a .58 caliber soft lead mini ball. Though it hit Pleasant's arm between his wrist and his elbow, it was of such brutal force that it knocked him backward from his kneeling position. Blood splattered as he fell hard to the ground.

Henry pulled him back out of the line of fire and called for medics. "I didn't have a chance to watch your back," Henry said, "but you'll be alright, Pleasant. See you later."

Medics rolled him onto a stretcher and carried him to a building on the outskirts of the town, which was set up as a makeshift field hospital. Even though it was early in the fight, stretcher bearers were coming in from all directions to the building. As they approached the hospital, Pleasant raised his head and saw a leg tossed out of a ground-floor window, landing on a small pile of amputated arms and legs. The smell coming from the building reminded Pleasant of a slaughterhouse he once visited back home. Once inside, a doctor took one look at Pleasant's arm and pointed the bearers to a room used for operations. That was the room he saw from the outside. Pleasant pleaded with the doctor: "Please don't take it off!"

The doctor sighed and said, "Son, all of your bones were shattered beyond repair by that soft lead ball. We have to take it off or gangrene will set in and will kill you. Come, let's get on with it. Others are waiting."

A male nurse poured chloroform on a cloth placed over Pleasant's face. His right arm was taken off just below his elbow. Pleasant would be going home.

With other wounded men he was loaded on an ambulance wagon, which would take them northeast toward York. The jostling of the wagon woke Pleasant from his amnesia-induced sleep. He sat up and vomited violently into a bucket. Then he looked in horror at his arm and cried himself to sleep.

After two days by slow trains, the wounded arrived in Indianapolis and were taken to the City Hospital. They kept Pleasant for a week of observation before discharging him from the army. The stitches in his arm were holding, and the medics confirmed that the wound was not infected. Hundred's of men had been carried in, many with missing limbs. Some had terrible disfiguring facial wounds they would live with for the rest of their days. He cried again when he heard that Henry Hughes had been killed in the Peach Orchard debacle at Gettysburg. Pleasant wasn't there to watch Kokomo's back.

A message was sent to Libertyville and Pleasant's father, David, brought him home in his horse and buggy. Pleasant was depressed and very quiet. "Son," said David, "you still have your life, a strong left arm and two strong legs. Things will be fine." Pleasant looked across the seat of the buggy at his father, shook his head and smiled.

As they traveled home to Libertyville, they compared what they knew about the fight at Gettysburg. The battle lasted for two more days after Pleasant was wounded. Pleasant's regiment held the high ground until Meade's main force arrived. The next day they merged with other regiments and withstood a desperate, massive charge across open ground by the Confederates, led by General George Pickett. The Union army prevailed, but there were tens of thousands of casualties on both sides. Lee retreated back into Maryland and Meade did not pursue him. David heard from his courthouse-lawn friends that President Lincoln was not happy about that. He thought Meade might have ended the war by catching and defeating Lee again.

The army had provided few details in its message requesting that someone should come to take Pleasant home; only that he was wounded and discharged from the army. David's buggy pulled up to the beautiful framed house that Ben Brooks had built for Cass and Pleasant. Tying the horse to the hitching post, he helped Pleasant out of the buggy. David pulled on the bell cord and Cass opened the door. Before any words were spoken, Cass saw Pleasant's jacket sleeve pinned to his right shoulder. David caught her as she fainted and fell slowly to the floor. After he revived her, David left amid Cass' low wails. Cass was not crying for Pleasant but for herself. *I am now married to a deformed man,* she thought. She could not even bring herself to hug Pleasant. Finally she said, "Come in, Pleasant, we'll get you something to eat."

Ben told his daughter, "He can't be of much help to me anymore except maybe on the farm. He can't draw up my buildings. Can't even use a saw right."

Pleasant went to work helping his father, David, on the farm, learning to use his left arm for feeding the animals and holding the reins of the mules plowing the fields. After a while Ben rehired Pleasant to plow his acreage and do odd jobs that he could handle. As was her duty, Julie brought the fieldworkers sandwiches and water every day from the Brooks' house, but for Pleasant she brought a special meal. When Pleasant wasn't there, she told the other workers that Pleasant couldn't handle a sandwich with one hand; that it wasn't special treatment because he was a relative. Julie was seeing Sam Coulter, the storekeeper, but somehow it wasn't the same. She couldn't get Pleasant out of her mind. His war wound didn't matter. *He said he loved me and then married Cass*, she thought.

Several months went by and Cass delivered a baby boy, who they named John. Martha and Ben hired a wet nurse and then a nanny, who also did housework for Cass. Cass kept her distance from the baby and Pleasant. She could not bear to have Pleasant hold her with the nub of his severed arm, or "stump," as her father called it, so she slept in a separate room by herself. Baby John's crib was put in with the nanny, Lucinda. Lucinda was slow-witted, but reliable. Pleasant slept in the guest room.

Cass spent most of her time at her mother's house during the days that followed, and only went home in the evenings to help Lucinda prepare dinner for the family. She often took the daily train to and from Indianapolis with friends to shop.

Pleasant grew more morose and spent his spare time hunting. He learned quickly to shoot left-handed, steadying his rifle with the useful part of his right arm, and slowly his accuracy returned. He liked the deep woods, where he could pause, sit on a log, listen to the sounds of the forest, and just think. Often he wouldn't even fire his rifle. His dog, Shadow, was still his sidekick. When Peasant would sit on a log, depressed with the recent turn of events in his life, Shadow would sit very still and look at Pleasant with mournful eyes, as if he understood and wanted to help his melancholy friend. It seemed his baby son was the only good thing in his life besides his parents and Shadow. John was a good baby and Pleasant spent hours entertaining him in the absence of his mother. *Will this go on the rest of my life?* thought Pleasant.

Even Shadow would be affected by future events.

CHAPTER 6

UNEXPECTED EVENT

Matt Johnson and several other veterans got off the train at the Libertyville station. Attaching a small pack to his back, Matt walked slowly to his parents' house. James was in his fields and Mary was in her kitchen. Instead of just walking in, Matt thought he had better pull the bell cord at the door and step back. Mary opened the door and looked at the man's smiling face. She grabbed the door frame with one hand to steady herself. All she could manage, in a shaking voice, was, "We thought you were dead. They told us you were dead." Then she ran up to hug her lost son.

A neighbor had seen Matt walking from the train station and ran to bring James from the field. They couldn't help but stare at their son. Matt was emaciated. He had lost his baby face and was a far cry from the stocky, strong boy who left them more than two years ago. James and Matt sat around the kitchen table. Mary brought some food and drinks, and then sat with them.

After finishing his food, Matt began, "I was shot by some rebel at Stones River in Tennessee. I was crawling up a muddy, slippery bank and a ball tore through my scalp, almost taking off all the hair on the top of my head. I was knocked out for a long time, and must have been a bloody mess, I guess, since both our boys and the Confederates gave me up for dead. My head finally cleared and I could see that I was being dragged toward a mass grave, half full of bodies. Somebody was trying to pull my boots off! I yelled. They dropped me like a hot potato. One of the soldiers said, 'Well, I'll be dammed. This one's alive!' The Rebs half carried me to a surgeon's tent, where my head was cleaned and was covered with a crown of bandages. Then I was prodded by two guards into a fenced prisoner pen. I saw no one I knew. They were all sitting with their heads down. As night came the Rebs threw in some blankets and gave us a little food and water."

Matt's mother leaned over from her chair with tears in her eyes, and squeezed his hand. "My poor boy, that must have been awful," she said. Matt sighed, squeezed back, and continued.

"They marched us south from camp to camp, picking up more prisoners along the way. The weather got hot, but the food got scarcer. I watched the rebel soldiers marching the other way into battle. They looked as thin as rails. We figured they were running short on food, and that didn't bode well for us. A lot of them were barefooted, some with bloody feet. Those boys were allowed to walk in the grass along the side of the road. My shoes were almost gone when I saw one of my fellow prisoners, an older fella, fall dead in the scorching Tennessee sun. I tried to grab his shoes before any one else could, but I was knocked aside by a reb guard who threatened to kill me if I tried anything like that again.

Matt paused and looked at his parents. "Ma and Pa, I probably ought not to tell you these things, but I somehow need to let it out. I'm sorry."

Matt's mother got out of her chair and gave Matt a warm kiss on the cheek and another hug. "It's fine, son. We want to hear it all. We're just so happy you survived and are really home!"

"Weeks became months as we were moved out of Tennessee, into Alabama, then into Georgia. They wouldn't let us send letters and disciplined anyone who tried. The rebs tied the wrists of anyone who gave them trouble and stopped their food for two days. I wanted to let you know I was still alive, but I couldn't."

"We finally got to the big, new prisoner camp near Andersonville, Georgia. It was crowded with Union prisoners, some twenty or thirty thousand, they said. Things were unbelievable at Andersonville. When we were marched through the gates, the first thing I saw was men who looked like walking skeletons covered with filth. The stench was really bad. Not far from the gate I could see them throwing wasted bodies into mass graves. Our daily ration of food was a teaspoon of salt, three tablespoons of beans, and about a half of a pint of unsifted cornmeal."

"I wouldn't drink the water because it came from the same little river used for sewage by the guard's quarters up on the hill. Fresh water was as valuable as gold. I caught what rainwater I could with my rubber ground cover and my tarp, and funneled it into jars and bottles that I found.

I hoarded my water and hid it in case there was no more rain coming. One time a scrawny prisoner saw me storing my water. I had to fight him off with a club I kept hidden. We lived like animals, just fighting to survive another day. I thought for sure I would soon die in that hellhole."

"I would have never survived," his father said, shifting in his chair.

Matt smiled. "You would, Pa, if you had to."

"Then, by chance, and maybe because of Ma's and Cass' prayers, a miracle happened," Matt continued. "At roll call one day, two rebel sergeants picked me and a few other prisoners out of the line, and told us to get our gear. They told us they were 'patrolling us.' That's what they call a prisoner exchange. I think they picked us 'cause we could still walk some. They rationed a little better food once we were out of that hellhole; fattened us up a bit for the exchange, we figured."

"It seemed like it took forever to get north again. I didn't care 'cause I wouldn't die at Andersonville. After what seemed like months, we made it to a prisoner exchange place somewhere south of Nashville. When I crossed that line to our waiting boys, I fell on my knees and thanked the Lord. They put me on a cot and a doc gave me some kind of medicine."

"After a week or so, they gave me some papers, and one of the docs told me, 'Your enlistment is sure up after all that time as a prisoner. Boy, you get on home.' "

"Ma, if you think I look bad now, you should've seen me at Andersonville. I really needed your corn bread and bacon."

They finished their meal and Matt stood up slowly, still not steady on his feet. "Thanks, Ma and Pa. Now I've got to get over to the Brooks' and see my girl."

There was dead silence. "Matt, sit down, please," his mother said. Reluctantly he took his seat. "Matt, we all thought you were dead. They said so, in writing, in an official letter delivered by some Union officer. I've got it in the drawer over there if you want to see it. So we cried and grieved you for weeks. Now listen, my dear boy, after a while Cass and Pleasant started taking up together. They were married about ten months ago. Matt, they have a fine baby boy, named John." She paused. "What's more you don't know is that Pleasant was shot at Gettysburg and lost most of his right arm."

Matt looked deeply into his mother's eyes, and then his father's. Both were crying. Matt was without words. He put his face in his hands, lowered his head to the table, and sobbed.

CHAPTER 7

PROBLEMS

Cass maneuvered her buggy around a wagon full of corn on the road to her parents' house and tied her horse to the bridle post. She had been visiting a friend in nearby Sheridan. Her mother, Martha, ran out to meet her. "Cass, hold on to yourself. I've got unbelievable news! Matt Johnson has returned from the war! He is alive but needs fattening up, I hear. He has been in prisoner camps for more than a year or so and was part of a prisoner exchange."

Cass held her mother's shoulders in a vice grip and stared into her eyes. "Are you sure, Mother, are you really sure?"

"Yes, Cass, the James twins saw him walking home from the train and ran to greet him. They stopped in our house to tell us on their way home. The boys said he was skinny as a rail but was not limping or anything."

Cass moved toward a bench on the porch and sat down, shaking her head from side to side, trying to take it all in. Then she started sobbing softly. Martha sat next to her and held her until the sobs subsided. Suddenly Cass straightened, looked at her mother and said, "I will not let my life be ruined. Now, I must go see him."

Martha held Cass' hands firmly. "Cass, hold on, you have your own family now. What happened was terrible. This awful war has changed thousands of lives, including yours. Now take what's happened to you and leave well enough alone."

Cass wrested her hands away from Martha and stood. "Thank you, Mother. I understand what you are saying, but I'm determined to live my life as I see fit." She paused. "For now, I will think. Now I'd better go home and help Lucinda with supper."

It took some time for Mary to build up Matt's strength to where it was before he left more than two years ago. With improved health, Matt got his anger back as well. He first directed it toward the Union army for not declaring him missing and not necessarily dead. He also believed that eventually they should have at least listed him as a prisoner.

The Provost Marshall at the Libertyville County Courthouse listened patiently, and then said, "Son, in fierce battles like you were in, everything is chaotic. Terrible mistakes happen. The Confederates didn't care who you were. They'd sooner you be dead than have another mouth to feed. And they seldom make lists of prisoners. I guess they're too busy for that. They really don't give a damn. Now, I think you should thank God that you were patrolled out of Andersonville and are still alive! You have your whole life ahead of you, not like your fellow soldiers who died that day in Tennessee and many others who are still dying every day."

Matt sat for a minute, got up from his chair and said, "All right, sir. I suppose it's gonna take me a lot of time to get over this. Guess I'd better try."

Walking home from the Provost Marshall's office, Matt thought: *I guess I am lucky, except for what happened to my Cass.* He blamed Pleasant for marrying Cass, his fiancé, while he was away, regardless of what happened. *Why did Pleasant think I was, for sure, dead? There was no body! Why didn't he wait a decent time to make sure I was dead and not a prisoner? I thought Pleasant was my friend. We spent many good hours together on building projects. I thought I could trust him. I sure was wrong.* Matt couldn't leave well enough alone. He wanted Cass back.

CHAPTER 8

TROUBLES

The building projects had slowed because of the war, and Ben Brooks turned his attention to planting and harvesting more crops. A Union agent, who bought food for the army, approached Ben and convinced him to sell his crops at an inflated price to the government. The agent then received kickbacks from Ben. Both men enriched themselves as the war continued.

Ben welcomed Matt back and made him manager of his farm and the building business. Matt had to hold his grievance against Pleasant and had little to say to him as they ate their lunches with the field workers. Although Pleasant tried to draw him into conversation, Matt would walk away from him, saying he had to get back to work. Pleasant knew Matt was hurt by his marriage to Cass, but that was history, so Pleasant thought. He wondered if something unusually bad had happened to Matt at Stones River, or Andersonville, which Matt was trying to forget. *Each of us has his own ghosts from the war*, he thought. One of

Pleasant's qualities was that he never harbored resentment toward, or thought to seek revenge on, anyone in his life. And he thought, naively, that other people were about the same as him, and that they thought about the same as he did. Pleasant just turned nineteen, and had unusually kind and loving feelings toward his fellow man, probably to a fault.

James and Mary Johnson decided to celebrate Matt's return with a pig roast at their farm. It was a cool, fall day with a hint of the approaching winter in the air. They invited friends and family, including Pleasant and Cass White. It was a joyous occasion and hard apple cider and a little whiskey brought in by fellow veterans served to increase the laughter and back slapping. Matt had to tell his survival story several times to different groups of people. His tale would be carried through Libertyville County for weeks; each time embellished a bit more.

When Matt approached Pleasant and Cass, Pleasant said, "It was a miracle, Matt," and held out his left hand for a shake. Matt shook hands and managed to say, "Sorry about your arm." It was the first time Matt had acknowledged his wound. Matt hugged his former fiancé awkwardly as her eyes welled up. Cass could feel the eyes of everyone looking at them. There was a pause in conversations, which resumed quickly in nervous chatter as Matt, Cass, and Pleasant talked briefly of other things, including baby John.

Cass and Pleasant left the party early and, in silence, drove their buggy home. With only a side glance at Lucinda and a sleeping John, Cass went right to her room and closed the door.

After putting up the horse in the barn, Pleasant returned to the porch, sat down on the bench, and pulled a pint bottle of whiskey from his jacket pocket. An old farmer had slipped it into his pocket at the pig roast, saying, "Here's something for you, Pleasant. There was no pig roast for you. Welcome home!" He sipped on the whiskey and could not stop the tears from running down his cheeks. He went to his own room and slept a restless night.

When plowing with the mules one day, Pleasant was seized with cramps and nausea. He couldn't hold food down for long and ran a low-grade fever. The nanny tried beef broth and home remedies to settle his stomach. But nothing seemed to work. He lost weight and strength and his complexion paled. The local doctor, Sam Fitzgerald, figured he had contracted a disease from the war, but didn't know what it could be. He went to the Provost Marshall's office, who arranged to have Pleasant admitted to the National Home for Disabled Volunteer Soldiers at Dayton, Ohio. The center had a large hospital that treated the hundreds of sick and wounded Union soldiers streaming in from the southern battlefields. A national cemetery had been dedicated on the grounds near the hospital and was rapidly filling.

David made a bed for his son in his wagon and started for Dayton. No one saw him off except his mother. Lucinda said Cass was helping her mother can tomatoes. Daniel reached Dayton on the second day, stopping over in the border town of Richmond, Indiana. He had to half-carry Pleasant into a small hotel.

The doctor in the admissions area at the Dayton hospital, Peter Hughes, puzzled over Pleasant's condition.

He first thought it was cholera, but expressed his doubts aloud. The attending nurse by his side said, "Please forgive me, Doctor Hughes, but I have been watching and examining this man since he arrived, and I think I have seen these symptoms before; they are not something you would expect in a war hospital."

Doctor Hughes listened to her, shrugged his shoulders, and told her to go ahead with the treatment she suggested. He asked her to put him in one of the isolation rooms until they were sure. The doctor thanked the nurse, Jenny Ranson, and then had to move along as the number of arriving wounded was increasing. Jenny was young, but experienced. She had taken her training in her native Chicago and, after a year at a city hospital, volunteered for a term at the Dayton soldier's hospital.

Jenny went to the admissions waiting room and found the patient's father sitting with his face in his hands. She told him his son was very sick, that he would be kept in isolation, with no visitors, until they were sure about his condition. She advised David to return home to Indiana.

As he climbed onto his buckboard, he thought: *Poor Pleasant, first his arm and now this. He was such a happy boy.* He remembered the words of their recent patriot, Thomas Paine, and said aloud to the sky and God: *These are the times that try men's souls.* He and Olivia hadn't heard from their son, Joseph, for weeks, but their other son, Michael, had written from the Union front that he was well and "not to worry." David said to Olivia, "How not to worry? We had such a happy home before this damn war!"

CHAPTER 9

JENNY RANSON

Jenny Ranson and the other nurses were tending to a ward filled with wounded young men, most of them moaning in pain. The low moaning carried its own unique sound, not unlike the soft chanting emanating from a monastery in the early dawn. After tending to many of the men, Jenny stopped in Pleasant's isolation room. Not only was his critical illness a challenge to her, but she had convinced the doctor that she could help this man to live with her diagnosis and treatment. He was her responsibility now. Dr. Hughes approved of her use of British anti-lewisite, an antidote, and the nurse gave Pleasant a dosage every eight hours. When he was admitted to the hospital he was so weak he couldn't lift his head. Within two weeks he was able to sit up in bed and hold down food. Color slowly returned to his face.

One day Jenny sat next to Pleasant's bed and told him, "Pleasant, I want to tell you that you have had arsenic poisoning. Do you recall being exposed to it?"

Pleasant stared at her and said, "No, I don't know how that could have happened. Farmers use it to kill rats in their barns, but everybody is very careful with it."

"Well, sir," continued Jenny, "I've seen several cases of arsenic poisoning before, and it appears that you have ingested small amounts of arsenic over a period of time, not a large amount, which would have killed you in a day. Dr. Hughes agrees. You know, don't you, that women use very small amounts of arsenic to redden their cheeks to look healthier and prettier? Do you have any enemies? Anyone who would want you dead?" Other patients were waiting for medicine and fresh bandages and she had to leave. "Think about it, Pleasant."

Jenny was off duty the next day and got a much needed rest in the nurses' quarters of the hospital. Pleasant was able to stay in his little room since there were no other cases that required isolation. He was excited when she returned to his room. Her smile was all he needed to feel better. Jenny was by now more than a good friend. Pleasant thought she was beautiful. Her light brown hair, braided and pinned in a bun in the back, showed from under her nurse's cap. The nurses shortened their skirts and avoided wearing crinolines when on duty in order to get around in the narrow aisles of the ward.

"How are you feeling today, Pleasant?"

"Well, Jenny, I'm feeling better now that you're here." Jenny was used to the wounded and sick soldiers who, without their wives and sweethearts, fell in love with their nurses. But Pleasant was different. She was very fond of him.

"Jenny," Pleasant said, "I was thinking about what you asked me about my poisoning, if anyone wanted me dead?"

He told her about his wife, Cass, and her alienation from him after his coming home with his war wound. Even her father treated him with indifference, almost contempt, when he came to work without his working arm. "Things got even worse after Matt Johnson returned home." He told Jenny that Matt was Cass' fiancé, who was reported officially dead by the Union army. Cass and he married a short time later. Matt was not killed, he told her. Instead, he was a Confederate prisoner for more than a year, and was finally freed on a prisoner exchange. Jenny listened in wonder and then had to complete her rounds.

She returned later, eager to hear more. "I forgot to tell you, Jenny," Pleasant said, "that I was out hunting with my dog, Shadow, right before I got really sick. I was aiming at a squirrel in a tree when a bullet whizzed by my ear followed by its rifle's report. Shadow ran ahead and I walked as fast as I could through the tall corn stalks in the direction of the sound. I heard Shadow yelp, and I picked up my pace. I found Shadow lying there whimpering, with blood on his head. Somebody had struck him on the head, probably with a rifle butt. I carried Shadow back home and everybody in the family helped nurse him until he was well. I figured that it was some kid who fired accidentally, panicked, hit Shadow, and then ran off. But now I'm beginning to wonder. Maybe some people **are** out to get me!" Jenny could only squeeze his hand and nod.

Pleasant's mother wrote to him every week, but no letters came from Cass. Something in each of Olivia's letters was ominous. She closed each letter with, "Don't worry about baby John, I'm watching out for him. Love, Mother."

CHAPTER 10

LIBERTYVILLE RUMORS

Gossip travels fast in a small town like Libertyville. Susan Jacobs and her husband saw Cass and Matt Johnson in Bloomsdale, about ten miles away from home, in a park where the Wabash River winds southward. They were seated against a tree on the river bank, holding hands. Susan said the couple didn't see them as they left. This sighting was, of course, reported to Olivia.

Pleasant's father, David, told her not to believe gossip, that Susan and her husband might have been mistaken. Olivia knew better. Lucinda had let it slip to Olivia that Cass and Pleasant slept in separate bedrooms since his return, not just when he was taken sick. Olivia suspected this from her visits to see the baby. Olivia didn't know what to do. She cried herself to sleep every night, worrying about Pleasant, her grandson, and her other two boys still at war.

Jenny visited with Pleasant whenever she could, even when she was off duty. Pleasant had fallen in love with Jenny and hoped she felt the same about him. She told Pleasant that the arsenic was in all of his organs, and it would take more time for the anti-lewisite drug to neutralize it and leach it out of his body. He would stay in intensive care until he was completely out of danger.

"Do you really want to go home after you're better, Pleasant dear?" asked Jenny one evening. "It really doesn't sound like a nice place to be, if not downright dangerous. You don't sound wanted there."

Pleasant raised himself from his pillow, nodded and said, "What about my son, John?"

"I bet your mother already has plans to take care of him as long as necessary. Remember, she thought you were dying and she still thinks you're not out of danger."

Pleasant's strength was slowly returning. He could get himself in a wheelchair to be pushed around the hospital floors by neighborhood girls, who volunteered as nurses' aides. Some of the veterans, whose beds were nearest Pleasant's room, chided him about his "private room" and his "private nurse."

Pleasant asked Jenny for some drawing paper, and he practiced sketching with his left hand each day until he tired. After a while he was doing well with his renderings. He wondered if pitching horseshoes with his left hand in his youth had helped.

He was happy that the staff didn't need his isolation room since it gave him more privacy for sketching and talking to Jenny.

Word was sent to Libertyville that Pleasant was still seriously ill, but out of isolation, and could see close relatives on a limited basis. It had been more than two months since he was admitted to the hospital.

Olivia and David were excited as they left for Dayton. Cass wouldn't go, saying she had to take care of John. Olivia chuffed at that. "Cass has a live-in nanny to take care of John." As they were leaving Libertyville in their buggy, Ben Brooks, on horseback, caught up with them. He retrieved two small, well-padded packages from his saddlebags and passed them to Olivia. "There was a fudge-making party at our house yesterday," he said. "Everyone pitched in: Cass, Julie, Martha, Matt, and even Julie's beau, Sam Cotter and me. One package is for you for your trip. The other is marked with Pleasant's name. Don't you go eatin' Pleasant's now! Well, have a safe trip!"

They stayed overnight in Richmond and arrived midday at the hospital. A frail Pleasant was sitting up in bed. Olivia cried when she saw him. "Oh, my son, we missed you so!" They updated Pleasant on happenings in Libertyville. They brought with them a recent picture of John, and Pleasant marveled over the way he had grown. His brother, Michael, had a two-week leave and then had to return to his unit in West Virginia. They also finally heard from Joseph. He had taken a wound to his leg but stayed with his company, now in Tennessee.

Jenny came by on her rounds, and Pleasant introduced her as "the nurse who is taking wonderful care of me." They asked her about Pleasant's sickness but she avoided a straight answer. After awhile it was time to leave and David started toward the door, then turned and said, "Oh,

I almost forgot a gift of fudge from the Brooks' family. Ben Brooks caught us when we were leaving. He said they had a big fudge-making party a few days ago. He said everybody had a hand in it. Made a special package for you, son."
There were hugs all around, and David and Olivia left for Indiana.

Jenny stared at the package, and then frowned.

CHAPTER 11

JENNY TAKES CHARGE

"I don't want you eating any of that fudge, Pleasant," said Jenny. "I don't trust it. Besides, it wouldn't be good for your stomach even if it was good fudge." They talked awhile about his parents, little John, and his brothers, then Jenny gave Pleasant a tender kiss and left, taking the package of fudge with her. She still had another round to make on the first floor before quitting for the day. The sun was fading in the west when she finally made her way to the nurses' quarters.

Jenny was at Pleasant's bedside early the next day. "Pleasant, let's get you into a wheelchair right now. I need to show you something." She pushed the wheelchair down the second floor hallway to an alcove and moved him as close as possible to a window. "That's the hospital's trash area below. Scavengers and varmints are attracted by the smell of old, bloody bandages and garbage, even though the containers are covered. Large blackbirds are usually about. Last night I opened your fudge package and laid pieces near those containers. Pleasant, look down!" There were several dead crows lying there along with two large, dead rats and a small raccoon. "Pleasant, I saved a good-size piece, which I took to our lab this morning. They did a standard test and confirmed that the fudge was laced with arsenic. Here's their report."

Pleasant gripped the arms of his wheelchair, looking down at the dead creatures, then up at Jenny's worried face, then down again at the trash area. He shook his head; there was disbelief on his face. "I might be dead now had I ate that fudge. My own parents brought me that!"

"Pleasant," Jenny said, "they said that Ben gave it to them when they were leaving. Your parents couldn't know that it was poisoned. I remember you telling me about Ben, your father-in-law, who treated you badly when you returned wounded."

There was a pause as Pleasant pondered all of this. "I never hurt anyone on purpose," he finally said. "I've been as honest as I can be with people. Why is this happening to me?"

Jenny was quiet as she wheeled Pleasant back to his room. She helped him back into bed, held his face in her two hands, and said, "Pleasant, you are a good, sweet man. And smart! I know, because I wouldn't have fallen in love with you if you were otherwise. Now, try to get some rest. I've got to walk the rounds with Dr. Hughes. We'll work something out. I'll be back later, my love."

Jenny had considered getting Dr. Hughes involved in what she considered attempted murder, but he was working tirelessly trying to save dying men's lives. In a terrible war such as this, evil happenings on the home front are displaced and mitigated with the awfulness of dead and wounded husbands, fathers, and sons. *I can't go to him with this,* she thought. *I will figure things out.* She couldn't believe that anyone would try, not once, but twice and maybe more times, to kill a wounded veteran. But she couldn't dismiss the awful evidence.

Jenny came back the next day to Pleasant's room. "Pleasant, they may try to kill you again. They are persistent. We don't know whether it is one person or more, but I have worked out a plan that can keep you safe regardless." Jenny looked around to make sure no one was around and lowered her voice. She told Pleasant that there was a small building on the edge of the hospital's graveyard where they prepared corpses for burial. There they embalmed them, dressed each body in a blue uniform, and carted the bodies to assigned plots for burial.

Jenny told Pleasant she would give him a safe sedative, which would slow his respiration and heart rate. His body temperature would drop a bit and he would appear dead. She said she would have two orderlies carry him to the preparatory building. "Your death papers will be pinned to your shirt, signed by me, since Dr. Hughes will be on leave and the other doctors are overwhelmed by all of the incoming casualties. Dr. Hughes knows you were still in intensive care, and he won't care if I sign the death certificate."

"I have been to the prep building several times," Jenny continued, "and I know their routine. When we arrive at the building I will dismiss the men who carried you. The burial medics take their lunch break at one o'clock. That's when we'll be there—shortly after they leave the building. There may be four or more bodies there waiting for prep.

They put them on ice, if they can get it, until they're ready for them. I will pin your papers to a body and remove his. The place is so busy and a bit chaotic, so no one would notice if there is a mix-up. There are more than six hundred patients in this hospital now. And, save their souls, most of them are dying."

"Don't worry. I will be with you at all times. My smelling salts will revive you, and then I'll slip you into a soldier's uniform. You'll be fine to walk to a nearby hitching post, where my friend Mary will be waiting with a horse and buggy. I will have all your personal things packed. Mary will take us to the Dayton train station. Then she'll take the papers to the office where Janet will make the necessary changes. They know what to do. That will also be the last day of my term of volunteering and I will have said my goodbyes to all. Then we're off! Are you game, Pleasant?"

CHAPTER 12

BUSY IN LIBERTYVILLE

Cass went to her father's office and sat down across from him at his mammoth mahogany desk. Lighting a cigar, he leaned back in his executive chair. "Well, what's on your mind, Cass? Something devious, I'll wager."

"Father," Cass began, "you must know that I love Matt and I don't love Pleasant. I married him because I was desperate. It appears Pleasant is going to survive his illness. So I want out of this marriage as soon as possible. Please pull some strings at the courthouse to get me a fast divorce. I know I won't be popular in Libertyville, divorcing a wounded and sick veteran. And Julie said people know I have been seeing Matt. That's why Matt and I want to leave Indiana right away for the West. We hear the Federal government is granting homestead shares in Kansas now that the war seems to be winding down a bit. They just changed the law so that former soldiers with two years' service can take title of one hundred sixty acres after just one year of improving your homestead. That's a lot of land! We can get married on our way."

Ben put his cigar in an ashtray and leaned forward. "Cass, are you sure about all of this?" he asked. "You would be giving up your mother and me, and a pretty good life, for the unknown. And I would be losing my best foreman." He paused. "You would get to take John with you. The woman always gets custody."

"I don't want John," Cass said. "Matt and I want our own children. Olivia and Lucinda can take care of John until Pleasant gets home. You can pay for the nanny for Olivia as you have for me. They'll all be fine. Someday I might get back to Libertyville and take my place as the grand lady of the county. When enough time passes, people forgive or forget."

Ben smiled a knowing smile and said, "Pleasant wouldn't die to make it easy for us, would he? You and Matt have been thinking a lot about this, haven't you? Do your mother and Julie know?"

"No, Father," she said, "but it will be no big surprise to them, especially Julie."

"The trouble with you, Cass, is that you're too much like me. When people and things get in your way, you fig-ure out some clever way to get what you want."

Cass smiled, shrugged her shoulders and said, "Another thing, Father, we will need a good stake from you for our trip and enough to build a house and outfit the place for a farm and ranch. I remember hearing that Mother's family staked you two very well, so you could move, buy good land in Indiana, and start a business. Will you do that for me and Matt?"

Ben sighed and laid his hands down on his desk. "You don't ask for much do you, Cass?" He picked up his cigar, leaned back, and finally said, "Okay, I'll help you. I think I can get a divorce decree in a week or less if I can persuade the right people at the courthouse. I'll work on getting your stake together. The trains will take you to Kansas City and I can wire money to a Kansas City bank. I think that's where you start overland, but I'll check. You'll need a large covered wagon and a team to get you there along with food and weapons for protection. It could be a long way from Kansas City to your claim that you are assigned."

The divorce papers were ready in three days. Judge Paul Sherwood was most cooperative when Ben slid a sealed envelope across the judge's desk. He granted an uncontested divorce by having his notary make a printed signature for Pleasant, because, according to Ben, Pleasant was too ill to sign. Ben told the judge to wait for his word before sending papers to Pleasant. He stopped by Cass' house and told her, "You're free!"

Cass braced herself for a visit to David and Olivia White's house. They invited her into their small sitting room and took seats. "I have to bring you news that may or may not shock you, Cass said. I have divorced Pleasant. I didn't really love him and that made things worse for him. We were no longer living as man and wife after he returned from the war. I'm sorry for Pleasant but I must live my own life. I'm leaving, too."

"How can you do this when he is so sick?" Olivia cried. "You are a terrible woman, Cass!"

"Maybe so," said Cass, "but I know what I want to do. I'm moving out to Kansas with Matt Johnson."

"Oh—my—God," wailed Olivia.

"What about John?" asked David.

"I'm leaving him here. The West is no place for a small child. I'm asking you to take John. He will have the same nanny to care for him. My father has agreed to pay Lucinda as before. I'm leaving my share of the house to Pleasant. Yesterday I signed a quit claim deed to give him full ownership. We will be taking a few pieces of furniture from the house for our starter place. Father will have them shipped out, but there will be plenty for Pleasant to use, if and when he returns. If he doesn't return, the house is John's."

David stood behind Olivia, holding her shaking shoulders. "You've thought of everything, haven't you, Cass, except the happiness of others. I've never used these words before, but you are a spoiled, heartless, bitch! Now get out of our house and never return!" Cass smiled, turned on her heels and left.

CHAPTER 13

ARE YOU GAME, PLEASANT?

Pleasant had doubts. "I don't know, Jenny," he said. "You have this well planned and maybe it will work. But what if it doesn't?"

"If we get caught we'll bluff our way out and say it was a dumb paperwork mix-up," Jenny said. "No crime will have been committed."

"Where will we go?" asked Pleasant.

"Evanston, just north of Chicago, is our final destination. We will stay with my family. You will stay at my brother's house and I will be down the street at my parent's house. I know you're still married. We'll cross that bridge later. I've written my family about you and the danger you are in. I didn't explain it fully; they probably think there is a demented patient who is trying to kill you. I couldn't very well tell them it is probably your wife, your in-laws, or who knows who else. Some day we will find out."

"This is incredible," said Pleasant. "I will be legally dead and buried. Who will I be? I will have no name!"

"Yes, you will, Pleasant," Jenny said. "I had papers made up discharging one Pleasant White from the hospital. Another mess-up in the hospital office if it comes to that. You also have your military discharge papers. You will still be Pleasant White, dead **and** alive, so to speak, but soon to disappear for awhile. We go on Friday, which is two days from now, so don't look so lively. Close your eyes and join the moaning. I'll drop a hint to the boys outside your room that you've taken a turn for the worse."

"We will take the train from Dayton to Richmond," Jenny continued. "We'll transfer to a new train route from Richmond to Chicago. It goes through Lafayette, Indiana. I will have a basket full of food with plenty of water. We'll be fine, my love."

Friday arrived and Pleasant was carried out of his room. Jenny walked alongside the stretcher, pretending to hold back her sobs. They went down the stairway and out the door toward the cemetery. Except for five bodies, the prep building was empty. She dismissed the stretcher bearers, and quickly switched the death papers. They were running late, and Jenny hurried to revive Pleasant and get him into a uniform and shoes and out the door. They were about twenty yards from the building when she saw the medical technicians on the hillside returning from lunch. She steadied a groggy Pleasant and they walked the other way without looking back. Mary helped her lift Pleasant up and onto the buggy seat. Mary took them to the train station and soon they were on their way to Chicago. It took several hours for Pleasant to sleep off the sedative. When he awoke, Jenny comforted him and said, "Here we are, Pleasant, away from your dangers! And what a beautiful summer day it is!"

CHAPTER 14

A LETTER FROM THE HOSPITAL

The postal delivery man rode up to Cass' house as she and Matt waited on the porch for Ben and Martha to take them to the train station. The postman's smirk and silence was typical in Libertyville now because she had divorced a severely wounded and sick veteran. Word got around quickly. *I'm ready to go*, thought Cass. One of the letters was from the National Home for Disabled Volunteer Soldiers in Dayton, Ohio, stating that her husband, Pleasant D. White, had died on June 21, 1864. The cause of death was listed as chronic nephritis. "What's that?" asked Matt.

"I believe that's kidney disease," said Cass. "Well now, he died two days before the divorce was final, so I should be getting a widow's pension from the government."

The letter noted that he had been buried in the National Cemetery in Dayton, Section H, Row 8, Grave 24. If a survivor wanted the person moved, there would be a $10 charge to exhume the body. Transportation to another site would be the survivor's responsibility.

"He can stay there," said Cass.

Ben, Martha, and Julie arrived in a large buckboard to handle their luggage. They entered the house, where Cass read the death notice to them. "It's hard to believe that Pleasant is dead," Ben said.

"I will have a hand copy made of this and mail it to the White's," Martha said. "I can't take it to them. Then I'll mail the original to you, Cass. Maybe I'd better have an extra copy made and saved, in case there is trouble with mail delivery out there. Is that agreeable with you?"

"Yes, Mother, thank you."

They arrived at the Libertyville train station in the afternoon in time for the three o'clock train to Indianapolis, the first leg of their journey to St. Louis. James and Mary Johnson met them there. "Martha, this reminds me of our big trip from Maine to Indiana," said Ben. "I guess it's in the family blood to try something new."

He pulled Cass aside and said, "Well, you've had your way, Cass. You're full of trouble, daughter. Now make a new life and cause no more trouble. Here's the letter introducing you to the First National Bank in Kansas City. A sizable account has been set up in your name. Telegraph me if you need more." Turning to Matt, he said, "Son, get some Spencer rifles, none of those muzzle-loading relics you had in the army."

Julie hugged Cass and said, "You're free now, Cass, make the most of it." There were more hugs all around and then they boarded the train, waving as they went up the train steps. Martha and Mary cried openly. "I have a feeling that I will never see them again," Mary said.

Olivia and David were shocked to receive the notice of Pleasant's death. They sat together holding hands in stunned silence. Finally the tears came. "I don't understand, Olivia," David said. "He seemed to be getting better. I think we should ride down to Dayton and visit his grave. Maybe we can talk to his nurse, Jenny, to find out what happened."

There was a stretch of cooler summer, so David and Olivia decided to use their buggy to travel to Dayton. They were surprised to see so many stone markers in the National Cemetery. The cemetery office supervisor told them there were two thousand, three hundred new graves dug in the last two months. He offered his condolences and gave them a map to Pleasant's grave.

The small, white, headstone read, "PLEASANT WHITE, CO E., 136TH, IND," with the date of death on the back. David and Olivia knelt on the ground and prayed for their youngest son.

"This rotten war caused all of his misery," said David.

"Let's not move him, David." Olivia said. "Let him stay with his fellows."

They went to the office in search of the nurse, Jenny, but found that she had finished her voluntary tour of duty. It was their policy not to give addresses of nurses or doctors.

"We'll visit his grave whenever we can," said David.

CHAPTER 15

A TRAIN RIDE

The Indiana train rumbled into Chicago's Randolph Street Station on time, where Pleasant and Jenny were greeted by Jenny's older brother, Trent, who was finishing his medical residency at Chicago's Mercy Hospital. He and his family lived in nearby Evanston, not far from Jenny's family home.

As they rode in Trent's buggy north along the shores of Lake Michigan, Jenny told Trent about Pleasant's survival from the war and then his near-fatal arsenic poisoning. Trent was familiar with the British anti-lewisite treatment. He looked over at Pleasant in his ill-fitting soldier's uniform, its right sleeve pinned to his shoulder. "It's time your luck should change," he said. "Pleasant, we'll do our best to make it happen. One easy thing we can do right away is to get you out of that uniform and into some civilian clothes. You're about my size, so that's no problem."

They arrived at Trent's house and, as he tied up the horse, Pleasant marveled at the size of their residence. "Father built it for Trent and Cathy as a wedding gift,"

Jenny said. "He's a building contractor and quite successful. You'll meet him and Mother soon. This is a large house
for Trent, Cathy, and their baby, so there's plenty of room
for you. They also have a housekeeper who cooks, so you're
no imposition."

Cathy greeted Pleasant with the same warm welcome
as Trent's. "I feel we know a lot about you from Jenny's
letters. We will be proud to have you stay with us," Cathy
said.

The next day was Sunday, and they were all invited over
for dinner at Jenny's family home. Peter Ranson was taller
than Trent and Pleasant, and sported a walrus mustache
that turned up sharply at its ends. Soft-spoken Margaret
Ranson was gracious and kind. Pleasant soon felt quite
at home. A glass of red wine brought a glow to Pleasant's
cheeks, and his gift for storytelling was restored. The
Ranson's were enthralled as Pleasant told them about army
life and Gettysburg.

After dinner, Peter invited Pleasant and Trent into his
study for fine Cuban cigars and brandy. "Pleasant," said
Peter, "Jenny told me that you have experience with a
building contractor back home and have a talent in drawing elevations and floor plans for buildings." He paused as
he drew on his cigar. "I work closely with an architect by
the name of William LeBaron. He has an excellent reputa-
tion in the Chicago area and is said to be a good teacher. If
you are in agreement, I think I can get William to take you
on as an apprentice. Well, who knows? He may get some
fresh ideas from a lad from Indiana!"

Pleasant and Jenny swung slowly on a porch swing at
the Ranson's before he left for Trent's house. They were both

excited about Pleasant's prospects at the LeBaron firm. "It's like a dream come true," said Pleasant.

"Pleasant, you still look troubled. What is it?" asked Jenny.

"I've got to know what's going on back in Libertyville," Pleasant said. "My death notice must have been delivered by now. I have a great friend, Jim Bartlett, who can keep our secret and let me know how my parents and little John are doing. Jim is a loyal and true friend. I'm going to write to him tonight."

William LeBaron was pleased to have Pleasant join his staff. It wasn't long before he recognized Pleasant's rare talent in structural design work, in addition to his sharp, concise artistic renderings in support of building proposals. LeBaron was experimenting with buildings supported by internal frames of iron and steel rather than masonry walls. At the time, buildings could only go two or three stories high, supported by massive masonry walls. Pleasant built a to-scale model, which served as a working developmental tool to study the statics and dynamics of various steel and iron internal configurations.

Pleasant finally received a reply from Jim Bartlett. It was "beyond belief" that Pleasant was alive, he wrote. He didn't understand what was going on, but he pledged to keep Pleasant's secret. His parents were still grieving Pleasant, and they had found his grave in the Dayton National Cemetery. "Please tell them soon, Pleasant!" They and Lucinda were tending to John, "who is a fine, healthy boy." The big news was that Cass had divorced Pleasant. Rumors around Libertyville had it that this was accomplished with the help of her father's chicanery, and that she had left Libertyville for Kansas with Matt Johnson. She did not want John. Jim also reported that both of Pleasant's brothers, Mike and Joseph, were due home any day.

Pleasant and Jenny talked for hours about Jim's letter. Jenny had never been to Libertyville and the only people she had met from there were Pleasant's parents on their visit to the hospital. Still, she had a vivid picture of his family and friends, thanks to Pleasant. Of course, both were happy that Cass had divorced Pleasant and left Libertyville. "So you are a single man again!" said Jenny. "Propose to me, Pleasant, so we can get married and provide a home for your John. Then he will be **our** John!"

CHAPTER 16

WESTWARD BOUND

Cass and Matt stayed two days in St. Louis to get married and see the city. The hotel manager found a justice of the peace and rounded up two hotel employees to act as witnesses. Cass wore her best dress, complete with crinolines and hoop skirt. Matt provided the wedding ring and flowers for Cass, and a local photographer took their wedding pictures and promised them prints before they left St. Louis. At dinner following the ceremony, Cass said, "Matt, I can't believe we are truly free. I love you so much."

"Cass," Matt said, "let's try our best to shut out the past. We are starting a real adventure together. Just the two of us."

Kansas City had the feel of a western cow town. After inquiries they found the Federal land grant office. Matt had his military discharge papers, which shortened the residency time to one year from the standard five years for clear ownership with deed of one hundred sixty acres of Kansas land under the Homestead Act of 1862. Their stake was in Cloud County, located in the north central part of Kansas. The agent finished preparing the grant papers and gave them two copies. He included a map that pinpointed the location of their claim. Peering over his spectacles, he said, "I hear there are hostile Indians in that county, but no matter **where** you go out there you can run into dangerous Indians and outlaws. Guess that's why the land is free."

He directed them to an outfitting company where they could get a covered wagon with a team of mules and all the provisions necessary for settling on their claim. He strongly suggested that they join a wagon train headed in that direction.

After a first visit to the outfitting company, Cass drew out enough money from the First National Bank to more than cover their needs. They bought a wagon, two mules, two horses, and two cows. Feed for the animals took up considerable space in the wagon. There wouldn't be much opportunity for them to graze as they moved with the wagon train. Matt loaded timber for building a shelter and tools for digging and planting. He also bought two Spencer repeating rifles, two Colt revolvers, and several boxes of ammunition.

They had to wait three days to join a wagon train headed northwest. The wagon master held a meeting with all of the settlers, laying out the rules of the wagon train, their route, and what they should do if attacked by Indians or outlaws. Cass was pleased to hear that eight of the forty wagons would still be together when they broke from the wagon train to head north for Cloud County.

They reached the border of Cloud County without incident, only to meet three covered wagons heading south.

Their leader climbed down from his wagon and walked slowly over to them. "Folks," he said, "we're leaving our claims because the Indian raids are too much for us. Three days ago they raided the Wood place, killed Joe Wood and his son, took their scalps, and carried off Jane Wood and her daughter. There's supposed to be Federal troops coming in a month or so, but we won't wait that long. If you go on, God be with you."

The eight families pulled their wagons together for a talk. After debate, they decided that they "didn't come as far as they had to turn around." They agreed to stay together until the soldiers came. Matt Johnson was the only man with fighting experience, so the families elected him captain. They went a few miles farther into Cloud County and set up camp on the left bank of the Republican River. They formed the wagons in a circle with the livestock, mules, and horses tethered in the middle. The wide river served as additional protection on one side. They pulled tables and timber from the wagons and made barricades with openings for shooting. Small holes were cut in the canvas covering the wagons to serve as concealed gun ports and rifles rested on the side board for a shooter lying in the wagon. Most of the wagons had repeating rifles, shotguns, and revolvers. They believed they were prepared for the worst. The men took turns keeping watch around the clock.

It was quiet for almost a week. Matt and another man rode out to scout the area and spotted small Indian parties in the distance. Still the Indians didn't attack. It was spring, and the wagon group decided to plant corn seeds in an open field near them so they might have corn ready for fall harvesting if the troops failed to arrive. During the day,

Matt assigned several of the men up to the hills overlooking the camp to guard, while the rest of the group planted the field. After the harvest, the corn husks would provide feed for their animals and fuel for their fires in the coming winter to supplement the firewood they were collecting. They ate fish from the river at almost every meal to save their other provisions. It was too dangerous to hunt for game with rifles, but they were able to catch rabbits and a few deer with traps and snares.

The Indians stepped up their raids in the beginning of summer as treaties were broken by the white man and Indians near the Nebraskan border. Tribes were now joining together in their fight against white settlers. No Federal troops arrived in Cloud County as promised. Matt was patrolling on a hillside when he saw a party of about one hundred warriors headed their way. He galloped back, shouting the alarm as he reached the camp. Everyone ran to their assigned positions, including women and children who could shoot. The Indians, Cheyenne and Kiowa, stopped on the top of the hill. Wearing war paint, many carried rifles too. Matt said to hold until he yelled "fire." He instructed them to aim for their bellies on the first shot when they were attacked, then their ponies on the second.

The Indians thundered down the hill, screaming their war cries. When they were about fifty yards out, Matt yelled, "fire!" The volley from the wagons knocked a dozen warriors from their ponies. With the second volley, another dozen had their ponies shot from under them. The horseless Indians jumped on the back of riders with ponies and retreated to regroup. Rather than another frontal attack, they rode to the left flank and galloped single file in front of the wagons, firing as they rode. The settlers' fire was relentless and more braves and ponies were taken down. Those now on foot rushed the barricades, brandishing tomahawks. They were shot down by both men and women with revolvers and shotguns. Cass killed one with her Colt revolver.

The Indians apparently had had enough for the time being and hurriedly collected what dead and wounded they could, and then retreated, disappearing over the hills. Matt rode his horse to the top of the hill to see if they were regrouping for another charge, but the raiding party had gone. Two men had been shot and another had a bad wound on his shoulder from a thrown tomahawk, but no one had life-threatening wounds. They posted lookouts around their perimeter, and then celebrated their defensive victory.

On the next day, Matt gathered their group together and urged them to form a militia since the Federal troops still had not arrived. Matt and five of his men rode out to surviving homesteaders enlisting help and, after several weeks, they had a group of eighty-five men on call. They organized what they named the 16th Kansas State Militia under homesteader Colonel James Banks, recently retired from the army, who had experience in the Indian wars. Matt was commissioned second in command under the colonel. In August, the militia decided to build a small fort for protection. Fort Banks was built near the settler's group of wagons on the river. After the blockhouse was finished, the militia began to patrol the area and many homesteaders returned to work their claims.

Federal troops finally arrived in the fall, manned the fort, and set up patrols. After harvesting their field of corn, the eight wagons left to tend to their claims. Following their map, Matt and Cass found the imbedded stone markers placed there by Federal surveyors long before the start of the Indian raids. Cass bought more lumber from enterprising merchants from Salina who, after they heard that the soldiers had finally arrived, hauled goods to sell to the homesteaders. Their prices were very high. Cass, remembering her father's tactics, negotiated lower prices by embarrassing the merchants for trying to gouge the homesteaders. She reminded them that after things settled down, the homesteaders would go to Salina to buy their goods from those businesses that had treated them fairly.

Winter was quickly approaching, and they hurried to build a small house with a fireplace, and shelters for the mules, horses, and cows. Settlers on nearby claims helped them with the building. Cass had watched Matt build houses and barns back in Libertyville, and she pitched in wherever she could. No more hoop skirts for Cass. She wore riding britches and leather chaps so she could mount and straddle a horse easily. A wide-brimmed hat protected her face from the harsh Kansas sun.

It was a chilly, late October evening, and Matt and Cass were sitting by the fire before bedtime. "We made it, Matt," Cass said. "On our own land! In our own house! Nothing or no one can make us move off of it, including those damn redskins." They had built firing ports around the perimeter of the house and covered them with sliding wooden slats.

CHAPTER 17

THE LETTER WRITERS

Pleasant was concerned that the shock of seeing him alive might kill one of his parents, so he wrote to tell them that he was alive and well. Pleasant rarely lied, and then only to avoid hurting other people's feelings, so he told his parents that there had been a paper mix-up in the hospital office, which caused the death notice, and that he was actually discharged from the hospital about the same time. The hardest part was explaining why he didn't come home. He couldn't tell them he was trying to avoid anymore arsenic poisoning in Libertyville, so instead he wrote that he had a "lingering weakness" and didn't want to be a burden on them. Jenny Ranson, the nurse they had met, he continued, had finished her term of volunteering and suggested he go with her to her family home in Evanston, just north of Chicago, where she could continue to care for him.

"I am now completely well and have obtained a fine position with an architectural firm here in Evanston. Jenny and I are in love and plan to marry soon. Then we'll bring little John to live with us," he wrote.

Pleasant apologized for not writing sooner, adding that he had exchanged letters with Jim Bartlett, who told him about the divorce. He asked his father to get a copy of the divorce decree and mail it to him. "I can't leave my new position yet," he added, "so I'll send you all train tickets to our wedding once we have the date set. It will be before the snow flies."

All of this news was almost too much for David and Olivia. They had just received word that their oldest son, Joseph, had perished in the Battle of Five Forks on April 1, just days before General Lee surrendered to General Grant at Appomattox. They had lost one son, but another had "risen from the dead."

Olivia wrote back to Pleasant with this sad news about Joseph, but expressed their joy that he was alive and that their other son, Michael, had arrived home safely. She added that John was old enough now to travel, and they looked forward to Evanston and the wedding. She enclosed a copy of the divorce decree with a note attached. "Good riddance!" it read.

Pleasant and Jenny were married in a large church that sat on a rise overlooking Lake Michigan. It was a beautiful wedding, attended by both families. The Ransons, long-established in Evanston, had family and friends who swelled the crowd.

Dr. Trent Ranson's gift was unique. He was now in private practice, and was also working with a firm that was developing prostheses for the tens of thousands of amputees who survived the war. He fitted Pleasant with a unit that was easily attached and supported by bands around his neck and shoulders. The arm was made of light balsam wood, and was moved easily by his upper arm. By now, Pleasant could use his left hand very well, but this "was a blessing," he told Trent. For a finishing touch, Jenny took Pleasant to a local artist, who matched his prosthetic to the skin color of his good left hand. The artist even gave him matching fingernails.

Three weeks later, after a short honeymoon in downtown Chicago, they traveled to Libertyville to pick up John to start his new life in Evanston. The family of Ben Brooks was not, of course, invited to the party for the newlyweds at the White's house. Jim Bartlett proposed a toast to Pleasant. "To our returning hero who lives again, this time with a beautiful new bride. We wish Pleasant, Jenny, and John, a wonderful life in Evanston. We hope they will return often to Libertyville, where they will always have family and friends who love them!"

By 1870, Pleasant was one of the leading architects at William LeBaron's firm. His design of a ten-story building using iron and steel supports for the superstructure won national recognition and awards.

John was now six years old and had a three-year-old sister, Helen, for a playmate. They lived in a fine home near the Ranson families, a wedding gift from Jenny's parents. Their life was an idyllic one along the shores of Lake Michigan, with boating on the lake, concerts in the park, and cultural activities at nearby Northwestern University. Jenny hired a nanny and took advanced medical courses at the university.

In October 1871, things changed dramatically for the White and Ranson families. A massive fire, which started in the south side of Chicago, was fanned by high winds and spread quickly to the central business district. The fire jumped the Chicago River and burned down thousands of homes and buildings on the north side. Scores of people were killed by the fire and hundreds of the injured, mostly burn victims, were transported to Evanston Hospital. Jenny and her physician brother, Trent, treated the injured for two days without rest. Tents were set up for the homeless all over Chicago. More than ninety-thousand people lost their homes in the firestorm.

Peter Ranson and William LeBaron came together in a sad meeting at Le Baron's home. Both had lost friends in the fire. "Bill," said Peter, "we were very lucky to have our company offices in Evanston. Many firms like ours lost all of their work-in-progress, as you know. It will be some time before the ruins are cleaned up. The insurance companies will be hit hard and many will fail. But as a result, Chicago will rise again with better, more fire-resistant buildings. In the meantime, we have those jobs in the Champaign area that will keep our men busy. Then there's the request from the State of Indiana to provide a consultant for the new Indiana Statehouse project. The consultant's role is to provide answers to technical questions from a committee which is forming and will meet for the first time next month. How about we send Pleasant? He's personable and is technically knowledgeable."

"Sounds good to me, Peter. Hey, I keep forgetting that Pleasant was born and raised in central Indiana. That might help in making friends, but then Pleasant has never met a stranger. You know, his work with the committee might give us a leg up when they get to the proposal stage."

Pleasant took the train from Chicago to Indianapolis to attend the first of weekly meetings of the committee held in an old downtown hotel near the proposed site of the new building. Pleasant and two engineers would serve as consultants.

The twelve-man, bipartisan committee was composed of leading citizens from various parts of Indiana. The consultants sat along the wall near the committee. Big egos were at stake, and each member seemed to think that the more boisterous he was, the more he contributed. Chairman William Marshall finally gained control by hammering his gavel on an old mahogany table. Before he could speak, Colonel Cletus Walker looked over his shoulder. "Who are those three men sitting along the wall spying on us?"

Cletus Walker was still fighting his Civil War, even though the war ended more than six years before when all wartime officers were sent home. He served as a full colonel in the Union Army, and still wanted to be called "Colonel". Now he was back being mayor of a small town in northern Indiana where he owned a general store and livery stable. While he once commanded thousands of soldiers, he now had only a few employees and a part-time city council to command. Word had travelled down to Indianapolis recently that he was abusive to his employees. In addition, it was said that the local sheriff put him in jail for two days after Walker repeatedly struck his wife while in a drunken rage. The townspeople didn't know what to do with their mayor, who was also their Civil War hero.

"Whoa, Colonel Walker, give me a chance!" said the Chairman. "These men are experienced people who the Governor and I invited to help us with any technical questions we may have.

"Gentlemen, will you please introduce yourselves?"

One older engineer was from the State Surveyor's office, and the other served as a building engineer for the City of Indianapolis. Pleasant stood and introduced himself as an architectural consultant from the Evanston firm of LeBaron and Ranson.

"Well, Mr. Pleasant White, you don't look hardly old enough to shave, let alone advise us on this major endeavor!" said Colonel Walker, causing muted chuckles among the members.

Chairman Marshall arose. "Mr. White is a senior member of a prestigious, well-established firm. He has received numerous awards from the National Institute of Architects, not only for his design work, but also for his construction innovations. His use of steel and iron reinforcements in the construction of masonry buildings is one of his major achievements."

"While this doesn't have anything to do with his architectural skills," Marshall continued, "Pleasant was born and raised in Libertyville, just north of here, and, what's more, he lost his arm at Gettysburg. We are pleased and honored to have him here."

A committee member next to Marshall stood. "Let's give him a 'hip, hip, hooray'." And they did just that.

Many of the committee members had little knowledge of building construction, and leaned heavily on the three advisors. Pleasant answered their questions deftly and thoroughly, and suggested other key issues the Committee might consider. One question from Pleasant provoked a lot of discussion. "Let's say you are standing three blocks east on Market Street. What should the new Statehouse look like from there?" One member suggested a square building with an atrium in the middle, filled with trees and a formal garden. Others wanted a more conventional edifice.

The meetings were progressing well, and budgets were set. Chairman Marshall suggested that there should be a contest for the design. Ten architectural firms were to be contacted and requested to submit building proposals. Marshall was about to close the meeting when the unexpected happened.

Colonel Cletus Walker reached into his kit next to his chair, and pulled out a Colt revolver. Everyone gasped. "Cletus, what's going on?" yelled Marshall from the end of the table.

"My wife left me, and my businesses are failing. No one wants to do business with me anymore," he spoke in soft tones. He rose from his chair, pushing it out of his way, and walked backwards a few paces with gun in hand. He eyed Pleasant, who sat along the wall with the two engineers, then looked back to the meeting table. Some members dived under the table. Others were frozen in their chairs at this unbelievable sight.

"Don't worry, I just don't want any of this to get on you," said Cletus. Then he put the barrel of the Colt in his mouth. Pleasant jumped from his chair, and tried to grab the gun with his good left hand, but he was too late. Cletus had pulled the trigger.

The Committee was recessed for three weeks to allow members to recover from what they had experienced. "Colonel Walker was another casualty from the war," Pleasant told Jenny. "He couldn't take the quiet life of his town after leading troops into battle, and witnessing the awful carnage."

After the committee meetings were resumed, four weeks were taken to evaluate building proposals. Pleasant recused himself from the evaluations since his firm was under consideration. After more presentations by the finalists, LeBaron and Ranson's firm was chosen, but on the condition that Pleasant White would supervise the final design and construction. Peter Ranson was reluctant to have his leading architect tied down to one project. He posed the question to Pleasant who said it was too big a project to turn down, but Pleasant also talked at length with Jenny, since they would have to move the family to Indianapolis.

"Pleasant, let's consider this another adventure," Jenny said. "I know some nurse friends who moved to Indianapolis and they love it. Our children are young enough that they will move easily. If we are optimistic and treat it like an adventure, our children will feel the same way. Besides, it's only a two-or-three hour train ride back and forth to Evanston to visit."

"Then we will make a good go at it," Pleasant responded. "It **will** be a new adventure. We can visit my family in Libertyville more often. And, who knows, we may finally find out who tried to kill me!"

CHAPTER 18

CHALLENGES

Times were hard for Cass and Matt that first winter on their one-hundred sixty acre homestead. The winter winds began howling in early November and continued for months.

They had stored as much food in the cellar as they could and had fresh milk from their cows. Cass remembered how Lucinda had allowed the cream to rise to the top of fresh milk. The cream was then separated and allowed to age for about twelve hours. She churned the cream until butter began to form. Matt enjoyed drinking the buttermilk left after churning.

Their attempt to preserve beef was less successful. A fellow homesteader gave them his "special process." They put the beef in a barrel and covered it with salt to draw out the blood and let it sit for a day. After draining it off, they poured in the preserving brine. When they wanted to eat the beef in winter, the brine was drained and the meat par-boiled. "Matt, please bring in your axe and the chopping block," said Cass. Cass used the blunt end of the axe and pounded the meat to try to tenderize it. That didn't help much.

"Cass, this stuff is as tough as boot leather, tougher than beef jerky," said Matt.

"Well, let's store it back in the barrel. It might be better than starving to death!"

The snow finally reached the roof of their small cabin. Matt kept a path opened in the deep snow to the livestock shed so he could feed them their daily ration of grain and corn husks, and to milk the cows. He kept a special watch on his mules. Without mules there would be no plowing and planting in the spring.

The Indian raids had subsided with the arrival of the Federal troops stationed at Fort Banks, about three miles away. The harsh winter was also a deterrent even to the hardy Indians. Their short-legged ponies were slow in the deep snow.

Spring finally arrived to Cloud County. Matt sharpened his plow blades and waited for the frozen ground to soften to allow him to plow and plant corn and wheat. Neighboring folks began visiting again and mail service resumed with some regularity. In April, they were shocked to learn from sister Julie that Pleasant was alive and well in Evanston. "I guess I can throw away that death certificate," Cass said. "I can't believe he really didn't die! The Federal hospital said he died!"

They also learned that the Civil War had finally ended. Robert E. Lee had surrendered his Confederate Army to General Grant at the Appomattox County Courthouse in Virginia. The settlers organized a barbecue to celebrate the bloody war's end. Matt was pleased to hear that the commandant of the Andersonville, Georgia, prison camp was hanged immediately by Union troops.

About that time, Cass and Matt were told by neighbors that a good number of homesteaders had abandoned their stakes because of the devastating winter and Indian raids. An option under the Homestead Act had allowed homesteaders to purchase the land from the government for $1.25 per acre after living on the land for six months, building a shelter, and working the land. Otherwise the wait for clear title was five years. Many had chosen this option and already owned their deeds. Now they were about to lose their investment by abandoning the land and heading "home," never to return. They had suffered enough hardship.

Cass wrote to the land grant office in Kansas City, inquiring if she could buy deeded land from the abandoning settlers. "Matt," Cass said, "I still have a lot of money in my Kansas City account. We could offer them $.60 per acre for clear title and see what happens. At least the settlers would have $96.00 rather than lose everything."

The Federal land office wrote back that they had no problem with her plan, authorized her to proceed, and provided forms, including bill-of-sale and quit-claim-deed transfer papers. The federal government did not want the land simply abandoned. Cass agreed that she and Matt would maintain the properties until resold.

Over the next few years, Cass acquired two-dozen pieces of abandoned homestead land, almost 4,000 acres. People were still pressing westward, so she sold several land parcels at a good profit and signed up a number of tenant farmers on other land, who paid her for farming her land.

There were also a few sharecroppers, who shared their crop yields with the Johnson's. She hired an attorney in Salina to set up a land-holding company. That led to the formation of a construction company to build houses and barns. Matt managed the company and its construction workers. Eventually they needed to hire a foreman and three hands for their own property, as their planted crops and cattle herd grew larger.

When many homesteaders abandoned their stakes, they took only as many horses and mules needed to get home, and opened their gates to let their livestock run free. They would be eaten by wolves and coyotes, or be taken by Indians. This livestock was collateral for bank loans given to homesteaders. Several banks in Salina and Kansas City contracted with Cass to round up and bring in abandoned cattle, hogs, horses, and mules. Cass and Matt put out the word that they needed hands to drive and cart the animals to Salina. Many settlers stopped improving their land long enough to make some needed cash.

Cass and Matt became very rich as the years progressed. She kept the money in her name in the Salina branch of her Kansas City bank. Matt didn't raise any questions about this; it was her money to start with and her ideas. "I can't figure the numbers like you can, Cass."

They were living well and had built the largest house in Cloud County. They also kept their original cabin, enlarged it, and fortified it to use as a blockhouse. Reports were circulated that the Cheyenne renegades were coming south out of Nebraska reservations and were again attacking settlers in Cloud County. The Indians would scout the movement of Federal patrols and then raid unprotected homes.

The Johnson's large, new house and growing cattle herd had been noticed by Cheyenne scouts, who reported this to Gray Fox, their murdering, renegade chief. One afternoon in May, Cass met with three sellers in her house office, who had decided they wanted no more of prairie life. The settlers believed they could do better if together they negotiated their sales prices. Cass listened for awhile, and then gave them her final offers. "Take it or leave it, gentlemen." They took her offers, cussing throughout the transactions. They finally rode off with checks in hand after reluctantly signing papers.

Cass was still filing the papers when their foreman frantically knocked on the door to tell her that an Indian party was approaching. They were less than a mile away. Cass told him to alert Matt in the barn and order the hands to take their positions as they had planned. Matt, Cass, and two hands manned port-holes in the blockhouse. The foreman and the other hand took positions behind the barn. All of the men had Spencer repeating rifles.

Cass counted nine warriors, all carrying rifles. Their bodies were adorned with war paint. With Gray Fox leading, they rode double file into the Johnson's yard. Cass opened the heavy blockhouse door, stepped outside, leaving the door ajar. She had a Colt revolver strapped to her leg under her leather skirt. "What do you want?" demanded Cass.

"I am Chief Gray Fox. I want you, pretty woman, and your cattle." Then with a sweep of his arm, he said, "Then we will burn all of your buildings. That big house will burn fast."

"Chief," Cass said, "There are many guns pointed at you. If you don't want to die, leave now!"

Gray Fox laughed. "We saw your men ride away. You are alone. Your guns poking out are just wooden sticks, carved and painted to look like rifles. Other white stealers of land tried the same trick. You lie like the Bluecoats!"

With that he moved his pony sideways and reached out to grab Cass. She turned quickly into the blockhouse, slamming and bolting the heavy door behind her. Shoving her Colt in the first porthole near the door, she fired two quick shots into Gray Fox's chest. Surprise was still in his eyes as he toppled off his pony. The men opened fire and caught the braves in a devastating crossfire. The warriors were shot several times before they fell from their ponies, getting off just a few wild shots before they died. The farm hands stacked the bodies behind the barn and rounded up the ponies. Matt sent one man to Fort Banks to tell the soldiers to bring a wagon to remove the bodies, and enough men to take the Indian's ponies.

Word traveled quickly around Cloud County and adjacent counties about the thwarted Indian raid and the demise of the murderer, Gray Fox. Cass Johnson's name became the stuff of folklore in Kansas territory.

The Indian raids became less of a threat in Cloud County as the tribes moved north and west into the Dakotas and Montana. A few years later, in 1876, General George Custer and two-hundred sixty-eight of his men were massacred near Little Bighorn River in Montana by a combined force of Lakota, Northern Cheyenne, and Arapaho tribes led by Crazy Horse. "If the government hadn't pushed them off their native land," Cass told Matt, "they wouldn't have been so revengeful."

All was well until another letter arrived some time later from Julie, with news that their father, Ben Brooks, had been arrested by Federal agents for war profiteering. She complained that a buying agent for the army "got religion" and confessed to taking kickbacks from Ben Brooks for paying inflated prices for his corn over a long period of time. Ben was sentenced to two years at the state prison in Michigan City, Indiana. He was also fined such a large amount that Martha had to sell their big house and half of their land. The stigma was too much for Martha. After her husband was led away in handcuffs, she moved back to Maine to live with her elderly, widowed mother.

Julie married Sam Coulter and gave birth to a son. She taught full time, but couldn't tolerate her students whispering about her "criminal father." Distraught, they sold their hardware store and moved to Indianapolis where they opened another store.

Cass sent money to her mother in Maine with a letter assuring her that after enough time passed, her father's dealings would be "forgotten or forgiven," and "not to despair."

CHAPTER 19

ANOTHER CHALLENGE

The Indiana Statehouse construction was a massive undertaking. Pleasant and his staff spent five years in its detailed design and construction, since many changes were made to accommodate politicians who wanted a bigger office or a better view. The Governor called Pleasant into his office at the old Statehouse. "Son, I hear those rascals are pressuring you for bigger offices," he said. "That's fine with me since we're still within budget, but I want to make sure that my office is twice as big as the biggest of theirs, since I have twice as much work to do than any of those carpet-baggers, and I **am** the governor!"

The architecture was influenced by the national Capital. Its style was classical Renaissance Revival, using a cruciform plan with a central domed rotunda. It was deemed a successful venture by Peter Ranson and William LeBaron, and was generally well accepted by the Indiana government and the citizens, though some of the officeholders and government staff were never satisfied with the size of their offices.

"Jenny, your mother and I hope you will soon move back to Evanston," wrote Peter Ranson. He was getting ready to retire and wanted Pleasant to take over the firm. However, Pleasant and Jenny were, by then, firmly established in Indianapolis and politely declined his offer. John and Helen attended good schools and had made lasting new friends. Their life in Evanston was forgotten by the children.

With Peter's blessing, Pleasant opened his own architectural and building company. The business grew steadily and his son, John, joined him after finishing civil engineering studies at Purdue University. Helen also went to Purdue and excelled in biological sciences.

John was almost a replication of his father with his lanky frame, his droll humor, and his quiet demeanor. He also had the understated magnetism of his father, and one day met his opposite in a lively, pretty Irish girl, Mary Dugan. After a long courtship and finally marriage, they proceeded with no delay to start a family.

Jenny had enrolled in additional medical courses at Indiana University's branch when they first moved to Indianapolis. Women were not yet accepted in medical schools in the Midwest, but Jenny formed a close professional relationship with two nurses and two male physicians. With Peter Ranson's financial backing, they formed a much-needed clinic for women on the north side of Indianapolis overlooking Fall Creek. It soon became the leading women's healthcare facility in the state. They named the facility Ranson Hospital after their benefactor,

Peter Ranson. Their daughter, Helen, was on her staff. She later married a young surgeon and raised a large family.

Pleasant and Jenny traveled often to Evanston and Libertyville to see their aging parents, brothers, and friends. In Libertyville, there was no one left who could offer any information about his sickness in 1863 except his elderly parents. Pleasant and Jenny decided not to tell family and friends that Pleasant had been poisoned. They saw no reason to distress them. "We may never know who tried to kill me," he said to Jenny.

CHAPTER 20

MORE SURPRISES

Cass and Matt discovered that they could not have children of their own, so Cass decided to try to get custody of her son, John, who was then nine years old. She hired an attorney in Kansas City who had connections in Indianapolis. The hearing was held in Indianapolis where the attorney represented Cass. Pleasant and his mother, Olivia, testified. His father, David, had passed away.

The court didn't take long to deny Cass' petition. Based upon testimony given, the judge noted that Cass had abandoned her baby son and left him in the care of Pleasant's parents. She had made no efforts to see the child in nine years. Cass' character was also in question, according to the judge, since she was seeing another man while her husband, a wounded Civil War veteran, was deathly ill in an army hospital. Pleasant testified that his wife never visited him in the hospital.

Other witnesses testified that John was in good health and doing very well with his father and his family in

Indianapolis. The judge saw no reason to change the boy's life, although he would grant Cass visiting rights if she would change her petition.

Cass shrugged her shoulders and sighed when her attorney told her the results of her custody petition. "I shouldn't be surprised," she told Matt. "I didn't treat John and Pleasant very well, to say the least. It was because I wanted to be with you. I make no apologies, but I'll let them be."

Then things turned for the worse in Cloud County as a plague of Rocky Mountain locusts flew in like thick, black clouds from the west. They caused great devastation in Kansas, Nebraska, and Missouri. One of Cass' neighbors had fifteen acres of corn ravished in three hours. Nothing like "The Year of the Locust, 1875" had been recorded before, and it shocked tens of thousands of hard working settlers.

Neither were the Johnson's fields spared, and were eaten to the ground by the insects. But they had maintained large storage granaries that were sealed, so they fared much better than the average homesteader.

The Johnson's shared much of their stored grain and corn with their neighbors, but many homesteaders just gave up. They had endured Kansas winters, tornados, a drought, and raiding Indians, but the locust plague was the final insult. Filling their wagons with their belongings, they headed back home. A number of settlers stopped at Cass' house and sold their land to her land company for traveling money. Cass and Matt held on and they grew even wealthier.

After the plague abated and crops were planted again and harvested, Cass and Matt decided to move to Kansas

City. Matt was getting older and was not as spry as before. That year in Confederate prisoner camps, particularly at Andersonville, had taken a physical and mental toll on him. They sold their farm and some acreage, and built a fine home in an elite part of the city called Strawberry Hill.

Cass' legendary exploits as a homesteader made her a welcome celebrity. She and Matt changed from their western clothes to fine dresses and suits. Cass had protected her face from the cruel Kansas sun with wide-brimmed hats, and she still was one of the prettiest ladies at social events. Her generous gifts to various charities gave her a big boost up in Kansas City society.

Cass' beloved Matt suffered a sudden massive heart attack and died at the age of forty-two. She was devastated. *I didn't even have a chance to say goodbye and tell him that I loved him very much,* she thought. Cass lost her desire to go on in business without Matt at her side, and she slowly sold off her vast real estate holdings in Cloud County and continued on as a wealthy widow. After a time, several of her friends attempted to match her up with eligible gentlemen. She allowed three men to court her, but decided none of them came close to her Matt. Each was rather well-to-do, but she still suspected fortune hunting. They all tended to be sycophants for the most part, and Cass was richer than all three put together. Instead, she decided to see the world and buttoned up her Kansas City mansion, leaving her bank's real estate department to watch over it. Cass was ready for a change, but never dreamed about what would happen next.

CHAPTER 21

ACROSS THE ATLANTIC

During the first few years Cass traveled around Europe, using Paris, her favorite city, as her base. She maintained a suite at the newly opened Ritz hotel located on the Vendome Plaza in the heart of Paris. She soon met lady friends at the hotel and they joined her in traveling on the European trains to new destinations. After a time, she picked up a working knowledge of the French language by immersing herself in the French culture and conversing with friends.

One evening Cass and a lady friend decided to dine at Maxim's, one of the finest, new, art nouveau restaurants in Paris. It was **the** place to go for wealthy Europeans. Stepping into Maxim's was an experience unparalleled. A myriad of sights and sounds vied for the attention of the entering patron: blue velvet drapery festively adorned with lace and ribbons; large antique vases overflowing with fresh flowers; classical music performed softly by a string quartet; and beautiful, bejeweled women, most of them with men who were well turned-out in tailcoats, waistcoats, and standing collars with white bow ties.

It was a busy night and they were seated along a mirrored wall in the main salon at a table for two. Seated next to them were an elderly lady and a handsome Frenchman about Cass' age. The tables were placed close enough that conversation was inevitable. The gentleman nodded, smiled, and introduced himself as Count Marc de Marshan and his lady companion as his aunt, dame Adele de Marshan. Cass introduced herself and her friend in French and said she was American. The Count then switched to English. His English was almost as good as Cass' French. They had a delightful evening trying to find the right words and pronunciations, switching back and forth from English to French.

The Count said he was recently widowed and lived near Bordeaux. He had decided to get away for a time to visit his aunt in Paris. As was the custom, he and Cass exchanged personal business cards at the evening's end. "Not that I didn't enjoy chatting with his aunt," Cass' friend said, "but I would rather have been in **your** chair!"

The Count called on Cass the next day to invite her to dinner. He met her in the lobby of the Ritz. Tall, slim, dark haired, and with a warm smile, he caught the eyes of several ladies sitting in the lobby. They knew who he was. There were no secrets among the expatriated wealthy ladies residing at the Ritz.

It was such a beautiful summer's night that they decided to stroll along the Seine River. From the Ritz, they walked down the Rue de la Paix, then through the Tuilenes Garden to the river promenade. They happened upon a river cruise boat ready to push off and they boarded. The cuisine was excellent, more than they bargained for. Cognac and coffee and the moonlight must have cast a spell, and they talked without stopping until the boat returned to the dock, continuing their conversation as they walked back to the hotel. They shared details about their marriages and the mutual tragedies of their spouses dying early in their lives. Matt had been taken suddenly, but Marc's wife suffered a long, debilitating illness.

Cass was so taken with the Count that it alarmed her, so the next day she asked her Paris banker to conduct an informal, quiet verification to ensure that the Count was genuine. He reported back in three days that the Count was indeed who he said he was. He came from a lineage of noblemen and had inherited his estate from his father, Count Pierre de Marshan. He was highly respected by his peers and owned a large estate, which included acres of quality vineyards. He paid his taxes on time and was kind to his employees.

That was good enough for Cass. She accepted his invitation to train to Bordeaux and spend the weekend at his Château Maria, named after his long-deceased mother. Cass brought a good friend, Jean, with her as her companion and chaperone.

The Count met the train at the station in Bordeaux, and had his chauffer tend to their bags. The chateau was large, grand, and dignified. Its horseshoe shape allowed for a long circular driveway. The manager of the estate, Monsieur Petain, and the head housekeeper, Mademoiselle Louise, greeted them cheerily at the front entrance. The massive double door was made of mahogany decorated with ornate carvings of armored soldiers.

Cass and Jean's accommodations were elegant and roomy, and furnished with raised canopied beds. Dinner was served in a spacious dining room enclosed with mirrored walls that made it seem even larger. Dazzling crystal chandeliers hung over a very long table. Marc and the ladies sat at one end of the table, which could seat some fifty guests. Cass wondered if Marc sat at the table alone each day, so she asked him just that. He laughed and said, "Good question. No, I usually take my meals in a small sunroom off of the kitchen. I'm only a count, not a king!"

During the three-day visit, Cass became enamored with Marc. On the train returning to Paris, Jean offered her unsolicited comments. "I don't know what you are looking for, Cass, maybe no one, but that man is elegant, kind, and funny. You would have to go far to find another like him."

Back in Paris, letters arrived from Marc almost daily. "I am smitten by you, Cass," he wrote, "I can't wait to see you again." He found reason to train to Paris often.

Another month went by and the romance flourished. Cass didn't think there would ever be any man who could take Matt's place, but she was changing her mind with each of his soft kisses and whisperings of love. Marc loved to laugh with her, and their contagious laughter amused the most aloof waiters in even the most exclusive restaurants.

A different time lay ahead.

CHAPTER 22

A NEW TITLE

The marriage took place in a small chapel in the artist's haven of Montmartre overlooking central Paris. It was a quiet, small ceremony followed by a reception with close friends at the Ritz.

They honeymooned in Venice at the San Cassiano, a fourteenth-century hotel located on the Grand Canal. They ventured out of their suite just once to take the obligatory but romantic gondola ride. The rest of their time was spent in a reawakening for both Marc and Cass. It had been such a long time for both that their love-making was almost insatiable. Marc was a passionate but considerate lover, taking his time to awaken Cass' dormant senses. Once awakened, Cass became the aggressor, leading Marc back to their bed until they both lay exhausted. Until now, Cass thought that her love life was over. Instead, a new world of loving, caring, and laughter opened up for Cass.

On the train back to Bordeaux, Marc reminded Cass that she was now Countess Cassandra de Marshan, and hoped that the new title would not change her from "his sweetheart and lover." Cass replied with a womanly laugh, "Only if you call me by that title in bed!"

The return to Chateau Maria was quite different from when she and her friend, Jean, first visited. Monsieur Petain and Mademoiselle Louise greeted her stiffly. "Welcome, Countess," they murmured simultaneously.

When Cass had told Marc of her businesses in America, he listened intently and was pleased that he had a helpmate with the management of the chateau's businesses. His deceased wife had been too ill during most of their marriage to be of help.

Marc's chateau was on the left bank of the Gironde estuary. His vineyards produced Cabernet based wines and also the sweet white wines, Sauterne and Barsac. Marc gave Cass a thorough tour of the vineyards over the first several days. She tasted a sample of each wine produced from the hillside vineyards, and over time she could call out the hill from where the grapes were grown.

She asked Marc who was responsible for keeping the accounting books for the wine business. Monsieur Petain kept all the books, he explained, and provided Marc with monthly results. He remarked that the business had lost money over the past several years, and he had to provide additional cash for its operations.

Cass asked if she could study the accounting details of the business, so Marc asked Petain to provide the books to the Countess. Petain laughed and said, "Certainly not, sir. A woman could not understand this accounting." Marc insisted, and Petain reluctantly handed them over.

On the second day of examining the books, Cass asked for invoices and receipts from suppliers of goods and services. He could not produce many documents. She also asked for a list of all the names of workers and house staff and what wages they were paid each month.

With Petain's list of employees, Cass went to the vineyards and told the foreman that she wanted to meet the workers. The foreman pointed out a number of names on the list who had never worked for the business.

Petain had set up nonexistent "ghost" employees and put their cash wages in his pocket. He also set up ghost suppliers of food and other services. He again paid himself and also Mademoiselle Louise, who was part of the thievery. When confronted by Marc, Cass, and the local gendarme, they both denied it at first, and then turned on each other. They were arrested and ordered to make restitution. Marc and Cass requested they not be jailed, but they were, of course, released from their employment.

The Chateau Maria's business soon turned profitable. Marc admitted he had been naïve to have trusted them, and thanked his Countess for saving their business.

After that episode, Marc held a grand banquet at the chateau to introduce his new Countess. It was a festive affair, and friends and neighbors filled all fifty seats at the chateau's mammoth table.

As time progressed, Cass and Marc considered the thievery of their staff small trouble compared to their next challenge.

CHAPTER 23

ANOTHER WAR FOR CASS?

France, like the rest of the European powers, had established colonies throughout the world, mostly by conquest. The subjected countries were now beginning to revolt to regain their independence. The French government was particularly concerned about losing their hold on French Algeria because of belligerent, unified Algerian tribes.

Marc told Cass that his father had sent him to military school and that he served two years as a lieutenant in the army after graduation. His father believed that because of their prosperity, Marc should give back to their country as he had done.

Soon a letter arrived from the French government ordering him to report for duty in thirty days. "Marc, why must you go?" Cass asked. "You are fine, youthful man, but you **are** a middle-aged man."

"I guess they need experienced officers, Cass," he said. "I must take my turn. I have no choice."

His commissioned rank would be that of Capitaine de Vaisseau. Marc explained to Cass that his rank was equivalent to a colonel in the American army. He was fitted in Bordeaux by an officer's tailor designated by the army. Red trousers with a blue coat had been the uniform since Napoleon's time. Cass fashioned a blue silk sash taken from one of her dresses, and tied it around his waist.

The night before Marc left, he and Cass made love tenderly and deliberately. It would have to last until he returned.

Cass pledged to take care of the chateau while he was gone, and made him promise to return. He assured her that he would return as soon as possible, yet Cass thought, *wars and more wars. Again my loved one goes off to fight. I hate wars!*

Marc's regiment sailed on a troop transport ship from Marseille across the Mediterranean Sea and disembarked at the Algerian port of Annaba. From there they made their way to the stronghold of the Algerian rebels near the city of Biskra. After probing action by his scouting patrols, Marc led the attack on horseback. Cannons and machine guns began their killing. The French took the stronghold and quelled the revolution, but they paid a heavy toll for the victory, including the loss of their gallant leader, Count de Marshan, who was killed by a shell burst.

When Cass received the notice of Marc's death she was inconsolable. She stayed in their bedroom for two days, taking no food, sitting in her chair weeping, with Marc's picture on her lap. *God is punishing me*, she thought. *He gives me a brief interlude of happiness, and then takes it away. I deserved this for all of my evil deeds. Pleasant's father was right when he called me a spoiled, heartless, bitch. How can I ever redeem myself?*

After Marc was buried with full military honors in the chateau's family cemetery, Cass decided she would return home to America. There were no real ties to France for her without Marc. She instructed her Paris bank to handle the sale of Chateau Maria and its vineyards. It took only a month before a neighboring noble bought the property.

Marc's will and testament left all of his estate to Cass as he had no other heirs. With all of the money from Marc's estate, she had her bank set up a charitable trust in perpetuity to benefit needy minor children of French soldiers who were killed in wars. Now she was ready to go back to America.

She reopened her mansion in Kansas City. It was not the same after being away for so many years. Most of her best friends had either moved or were now deceased. Her marriage to Marc had been reported in the local newspapers, and her remaining friends started greeting her as Countess. Cass decided she was no longer a countess. "I'm just Cass again," she told her friends.

Her home on Strawberry Hill was still full of memories of Matt, but now the memories were sweet and not sad. She even decided to visit their old homestead. Cass took the train to Salina and hired an auto and driver to take her north into Cloud County.

New roads had been built since she and Matt left, and it took some time to locate their homestead. The house and outbuildings were still there, standing strong against the ever-present prairie winds. She had the driver stop just outside a swing gate that was open. It looked like no one was home at the time, so she walked through the gate and wandered about for awhile, trying to bring back the hard times and also the good memories of their homesteading years. She walked to the blockhouse where she shot Gray Fox and shuddered at the thought of what happened that day.

On the train ride back to Kansas City, Cass looked out the window and thought about her life. *Well, that's enough looking back, now I will look forward!*

After many years in Kansas and France, Libertyville and Indiana now seemed remote to Cass. She wrote to an old friend in Indianapolis who confirmed Pleasant's successful career and family life in the city.

Her family was all gone now. After his release from prison for war profiteering, her father, Ben Brooks, had his remaining land sold in Libertyville without returning to the town. He joined Cass' mother, Martha, in Maine. Ben always had a soft spot for hard liquor, and that was his eventual undoing. He forgot he was not the bearish strong man of his youth and was killed with a broken beer bottle in a tavern brawl in Bangor. Martha lived to age sixty-seven and was buried in Maine next to Ben.

Cass' sister, Julie, had died giving birth to a third child at age thirty-nine, ironically at Jenny's women's hospital in Indianapolis. Cass was a widow again. And now she was aging and alone.

CHAPTER 24

JOHN TAKES HIS PLACE

Pleasant decided to give back to the State for his good fortune and turned over the management of his firm to his son, John, and volunteered for service with his political party. His warm personality and business acumen was welcomed, and he was elected to four terms as a state senator.

Over the years, Jenny and Pleasant received many honors from the state of Indiana for their contributions to the growth and prosperity of the state.

Jenny, the vivacious entrepreneur, and Pleasant, the gentle-hearted architect, died within two months of each other after thirty-five years of marriage. It was said that Pleasant died of a broken heart after Jenny passed away unexpectedly. His pretty nurse who saved his life in the Federal hospital was gone, and he just couldn't live without her. Their deaths were grieved by family, countless friends, and even strangers who benefited in some way from their largesse.

John and Mary White's three daughters, Abby, Jane, and Alice, took after their Irish mother, full of laughter and good cheer. Their large house was always full of friends, including new immigrants from the old country, Ireland. The White's helped the "greenhorns" find places to live and locate jobs.

Cass, now in her early seventies, heard from her friend that Pleasant had died some time ago. She decided to write to John to ask if she could visit him and his family. John never knew exactly what happened in Libertyville so many years ago, only that his parents were divorced and his mother moved to Kansas with a man named Matt Johnson. He heard through his Libertyville friends that Matt Johnson died and his mother married a French count named Marshan, who later was killed while serving in the French army. His father had chosen not to talk about her, but he heard that she was a shrewd business woman and had prospered in Kansas.

John was surprised by her letter, since she had never tried to contact him or see him after her custody petition was denied when he was nine years old. John had a forgiving heart and responded that they would be happy to have her visit. Mary and his daughters were full of curiosity about Cass. Dinnertime talk was filled with giddy speculation about what she would be like and how she would dress. "An older cowgirl, and probably mean," was Abby's guess.

"Remember, too, that she was a countess," Jane said. "I can't wait to meet her."

CHAPTER 25

THE VISITOR FROM THE WEST

John, Mary, and their three excited daughters gathered to meet Cass at the Union Station in downtown Indianapolis.

Cass had spent her last hour on the train wondering and worrying if she had made a terrible mistake by inviting herself to John's house. As the train hissed to a stop, she looked out of her window. John was standing with his family farther down on the platform. She knew it was him among the throng of greeters. John was Pleasant reincarnated. Frozen in her seat, it wasn't until the conductor touched her on her shoulder that she rose and collected her articles.

John scanned left and right, at people alighting from the train. He once saw a picture of what must have been his mother in the bottom of his father's Civil War haversack stored in the attic. He had rummaged in Pleasant's shoulder bag without his father's consent when he was about eight years old. He remembered how pretty she was; probably still in her teens at the time.

Now he saw her, the last person to get off of the train. The conductor held her arm as she stepped off the last step of the passenger car. There was a certain regal poise about her as she thanked the conductor and took her handbag from him. Her face was surprisingly youthful under her red-feathered hat.

"I think that is my mother walking this way," John told his family. He was at a loss about how to greet her. It was awkward. "Mrs. Marshan?" Cass smiled and said, "Yes." John introduced his family. Each of the girls gave a curtsy when they were introduced by their father. Tears welled in Cass' eyes and she warmly hugged each of the girls, John, and Mary. A porter retrieved her tapestry bags and carted them to John's new car, a beautiful white Oldsmobile sedan, a large car with ample room for all.

The White family home was on North Meridian, just fifteen minutes from Union Station. John had designed and built a magnificent house on six acres of land. There was a long drive with manicured greenery leading to a columned front portico. Because of its size, the house could have looked intimidating, but instead was welcoming. A parlor, library, and dining room led from a spacious foyer. A suspended staircase with balustrades curved upward to the second floor. Wings off the second floor led to a number of large bedrooms.

Before dinner that evening, Cass asked the family to open her gifts that she brought from Kansas City. There were lovely cameo broaches for her granddaughters and Mary, and a gold pocket watch for John. The family listened in awe as Cass told them tales of life on the plains of Kansas after the Civil War and before the Indians were pacified. Cass tried to turn the conversation, but her granddaughters were full of questions, and it was late when the family retired for the night.

It was a mild summer and the family enjoyed several delightful picnics on the banks of the White River and the Wabash River. The girls would get Cass to sing *In My Merry Oldsmobile, Yankee Doodle Dandy,* and *In the Good Old Summer Time* with them as they drove through the countryside.

While Cass was napping one day, the White family voted unanimously to invite Cass to live with them.

After returning to her lonely home in Kansas City, Cass decided to accept their offer. In fact, she hadn't felt so happy since before Marc was killed. *I will be a good mother and grandmother. This is my only family, I **must** be good,* she thought. *I've got a lot of making up to do.*

CHAPTER 26

A NEW LIFE

After advertising her beautiful mansion on Strawberry Hill, Cass sold it to a young cattle baron who insisted she include all of the furnishings. On her last night Cass sat in her parlor reminiscing about her times in the house with Matt, the grand dinner parties they held, and the festive holiday parties they attended together. Cass rarely cried, but she did that night, long and hard.

Abby, Jane, and Alice were delighted that Cass agreed to live with them. Cass had three large trunks filled with clothes and personal items that she brought to Indianapolis. The girls were excited and curious when they saw men bring her trunks from the station into the house. Each of the trunks was quite different. There was a large stagecoach trunk covered with tanned leather, which was highly tooled and inked. Another was made of blackened hide with brass bindings. A smaller trunk was bread-loaf shaped with leather straps, and decorated with large brass buttons.

There was nothing bashful about her granddaughters, and they begged their grandmother to show them what was in the trunks. "Everything in due time, girls," Cass said. "Everything in due time. Let me get settled and put a few things away." That was the last thing the girls wanted to hear, but their grandmother was not to be coerced.

Before bedtime they were successful in getting Cass to tell them more stories of life in the Wild West. She had to retell the time when the renegade chief, Gray Fox, tried to take her and burn their house down. They liked the part where Gray Fox got his comeuppance when Cass shot him dead.

They begged for stories about her life in Europe, the Chateau Maria, and Count Marc. These stories carried over night after night because of all the girls' requests for details. "When you met the Count," was one of their favorites.

She liked to read to them after they came home from school and on weekends. Cass' body was more fragile now, but she managed to sit ramrod straight in a high-back chair in the library with her granddaughters at her feet. She wore a Victorian, white-lace dress, with a high collar and puff sleeves. Cass read from *A Lady's Deportment,* the etiquette book from her girlhood years at Miss Adams' Finishing School. Some of the rules were outdated and brought giggles from the girls and smiles from Cass. Jane Austen's novels were favorites of the girls, and Cass would pass a book around and have each girl read a chapter "with feeling! I know that's hard to do with some of Miss Austen's characters, but let's try!"

During the day Cass wore her hair pinned up. Her lace collar and queenly poise reminded Abby of pictures and stories of the English Queen Eleanor of Aquitaine. At bed-time the girls would often rendezvous in Cass' bedroom in their nightgowns for hair brushing, a little gossip, and more stories from Cass. Cass looked quite different, and more youthful, with her long hair, now graying, cascading down to the middle of her back. The girls took turns brush-ing their grandmother's hair and she theirs.

Cass grew to love John's family and the love was mutual. John and Mary truly enjoyed her company and appreciated the positive effect she had on their daughters. Abby was more poised without losing her wonderful sense of humor. Jane's spontaneity was tempered a bit but she was still full of questions. Alice, at twelve, was Cass' favorite but she tried not to show it. Alice listened intently to every word Cass uttered, and liked to cuddle on the library sofa under a big afghan while Cass read her a story.

At holiday time, Cass showed the girls how to make raisin bread; a fun project yielding a dozen big loaves, most of which were taken to the church for the poor. Cass said she learned "the secret ingredients" from a Lithuanian immi-grant and homesteader who brought the holiday custom from her old country. It was a merry time in the kitchen, filled with laughter and chatter. Raisin Bread Day soon became a family tradition.

Cass had become very close to her granddaughters, and they often came individually to talk to her about boys, and how to approach their parents for permission to do special things.

It had been three years since Cass joined the White family. One evening before bedtime, she finally invited her granddaughters to see what was in her storage trunks.

The girls sat on her bedroom floor. Cass acted as dramatic as possible in opening the first trunk. Slowly, and one at a time, she took out beautiful ballroom gowns of different styles and colors. Cass had a story to go with each gown. A pretty blue gown with a plunging neckline was a favorite of the governor of Kansas, and he asked her to wear it again for him at a future event. Cass said he was a fine dancer for a governor and was a big flirt.

The second trunk was filled with undergarments, crinolines, and bone corsets. The girls had a great time with the corsets and tried to put them on under their nightgowns.

Finally Cass ceremoniously opened the last trunk, the one shaped like a loaf of bread. She reverently lifted out her leather riding skirt then put it on, wrapping it around her nightgown and fastening its belt with its silver buckle. She explained that it was slit down the side so she could swing her leg over her horse. Her riding britches were next; cut down from a pair of her husband's trousers and reconstructed. Her old cowboy hats had to be tried on by the girls. There was a leather wide-brimmed one for winter and a straw sombrero hat for the hot Kansas days.

Cass then located a picture of herself on horseback. The daguerreotype was faded a bit, but it was a hit with the girls. They asked to see pictures of Matt and Count Marshan. Cass reached for her large, tapestry handbag. She kept a small, silver-framed picture of Matt in a velvet bag tied with blue string at the top. It was a picture of him in his Union uniform. Another velvet bag followed. It was of Marc in his French officer's uniform with Cass' silk sash around his waist. The granddaughters agreed that they indeed were handsome, dashing men.

After answering more questions, Cass gently laid her treasures back in her trunks. Try as she might, Cass couldn't hold back her tears. Her granddaughters gathered Cass in a group hug and cried with her.

CHAPTER 27

REQUIEM

Time had taken its toll on Cass as the years rolled by, and she couldn't climb the long stairs any longer. John wished he had installed an elevator in the house, so instead, under mild protestations from Cass, he carried his mother up and down the stairs.

One evening John carried her to her room, settled her in her chair, and prepared to leave after wishing her a good night. "John, I must talk with you, please sit down and stay awhile," Cass said. "My son, I have done some terrible things in my life, and one of my most selfish, despicable sins was my abandoning you when you were a baby to go to Kansas. I was even too busy to care for you when you were a mere infant; I left that to Olivia and Lucinda."

"There is no way to make that up to you, John," she continued, "so I must ask for your forgiveness, which I really don't deserve. I'm so sorry, John!" she cried as she rose from her chair and almost fell to her knees. John reached out, pulled her to her feet and made her sit down.

"Mother, I was just a small child and remember none of this. You made sure, I'll wager, that Grandma Olivia and Lucinda were there for me." John pulled his chair closer to Cass and held her hands. "If you feel you need my forgiveness, you have it. I forgive you and pray that you will not let this trouble your soul anymore. You have brought your love to this house, and we all love you in return. Your granddaughters are maturing wonderfully with your thoughtful attention and lessons given in love. Mother, you bring joy and laughter to our family every day, much more than enough to atone for your perceived transgressions. Now, please, take your peace, Mother. It is well deserved."

The White family went to St. Brennan's Catholic Church. John became a Catholic when he married Mary, and Cass went to church with the family on a few occasions until she was not able to travel.

One day Cass asked John if he could have St. Brennan's Father Patrick O'Rourke "come by some time" to visit with her.

Father O'Rourke was a fortyish, curly-haired Irishman with a warm smile and manners that invited friendliness and confidence. They sat in an alcove in her bedroom, where the warm winter sun shown on a vase of red roses perched on a small, etched-glass table. As usual, Cass got right to the point. "Young man," she said, "I need to tell someone about some things I did in my life and ask for forgiveness before it is too late. I feel my body shutting down. I guess I need to be baptized and other things, but could you hurry a bit with the preliminaries? And, I have a hard time calling you 'Father,' since I'm probably twice your age."

"You call me Patrick and I'll call you Cass. Is that a deal?"

"It's a deal, Patrick," and on that they shook hands.

"I'll leave you these things to read, Cass, and I'll be back in three days, on Thursday, to baptize you. Okay?"

"I think I can last that long, Patrick."

He laughed heartily and said, "See you, Cass." Nobody called her Cass anymore. Now it was always "mother" or "grandmother." Somehow it made her feel like her younger self again.

Cass was propped up in her four poster, canopied bed when Patrick returned in three days. Her voice was weaker and her eyes were half-closed. Their family doctor had told John and Mary that Cass was going into congestive heart failure.

John and Mary witnessed her baptism and confirmation. "All of this in one day. A record for me!" laughed Father O'Rourke.

Cass smiled and whispered, "Me too."

Patrick smiled and said, "You stay well, my dear. We'll conduct the Sacrament of Penance tomorrow. That's confession, if you're willing."

"I'm not going any place and I'm willing. That's what this is all about, remember?"

Patrick arrived the next day and went into a closed-door session with Cass. He moved his chair close to her bed and put his stole around his neck. "This scarf means I'm on official church business," he explained.

"All right, Patrick, tell me again how this is confidential. I don't want my family knowing some things."

"I took vows as a priest never to reveal in any way what I hear in a confession. I am bound by the 'seal of confession', which is inviolable. You are confessing to God through me."

"All right, young man, I hope I don't burn your ears. I'll have to give you some background, so be patient."

She told him that she was a selfish, self-absorbed daughter of rich parents. Her mother, Martha, was an obsessive perfectionist and cultivated this in Cass and her sister, Julie. Her father was a hard-nosed builder who intimidated and bullied people to get what he wanted.

Her parents heartily approved of her fiancé, Matt. She told him how Matt had been called into the Union army and, after more than a year of absence, his family and Cass were notified that he was killed in battle.

Cass coughed and sipped on some water. "Are you with me, Patrick?"

"Yes, so far, Cass."

"Good, because here's where the bad things start."

After the notice of Matt's death, Cass said she charmed her sister's friend, Pleasant White, away from her and married him in a month's time, against her parent's protests. They were of the opinion that she married beneath her status because Pleasant was from an ordinary farm family. Cass explained that she felt no love for Pleasant; she was just paranoid about becoming a spinster, an old maid, because all the good young men were getting killed in the war. Then Pleasant was called to war, leaving her alone and pregnant.

"He came home from Gettysburg with half of his right arm gone. I couldn't stand to have him touch me with what was left of his arm, so I stayed in a separate room. I was awful to that poor boy. And I ignored our baby, John. I had a paid wet nurse and our housekeeper, Lucinda, along with Pleasant's mother, to take care of him. I went shopping or visiting with my friends instead of being a mother to my son."

Cass pulled her comforter higher to ward off the "chill," as she called it. Her breathing was ragged with short breaths. She would speak a sentence then pause to catch her breath.

"Take your time, Cass. I'm here to listen as long as it takes."

"Well, Patrick, we got a big surprise when my old fiancé, Matt, arrived in Libertyville quite alive." Cass told him that he was a Confederate prisoner for about a year after being reported dead. When she saw him at a wel-come-home party, she said their mutual love was still there.

"I talked at length with my mother about my dilemma. Divorce was almost unheard of in Libertyville, especially from a wounded veteran. Mother thought of another way to free me. She said that she would slowly poison Pleasant with arsenic. We would blame his sick-ness on a war time disease. Arsenic was easily obtained back then, you know. Women, including Mother, would take a pinch of it to flush their cheeks to make them look healthier. At first I was aghast, and then I went along with the idea. I wanted Matt so badly, I let her do it. We didn't tell Father, my sister Julie, or Matt. Looking back now, I know my mother was mentally unbalanced. She wanted everything absolutely perfect. As long as Pleasant was alive, and Matt was alive and available, her life was not perfect."

Lunches for the field workers on her parent's farm were prepared in their kitchen, Cass explained. Pleasant was working on the farm because of his disability. He had a special meal because he couldn't handle a sandwich very well. Martha would sprinkle the poison in his lunch food every day. Cass said her mother paid the cook at Cass' house, Lucinda, to add the powder to Pleasant's meal. Martha told Lucinda it was an aphrodisiac to help Pleasant's manhood.

Father O'Rourke looked at Cass incredulously. "I told you it was bad stuff," whispered Cass.

"When Pleasant was not getting sick fast enough for Mother, she followed him into the fields while he was hunting, and took a shot at him with her rifle. I didn't know she was going to do that. Most farm women could shoot and Mother was a good shot. But she missed him, and told me she had to strike his hunting dog with her rifle butt when it caught up with her. She slipped away through the tall corn. She was an obsessed, sick person. I must been close to that mindset. Mother later died in an insane asylum in Maine. I guess I barely avoided that."

She paused, had a coughing spell, and motioned to Patrick to hand her the water glass.

She sipped for a moment and smiled a thank you to Patrick.

"I **will** get through this," Cass said, with as much strength in her voice as she could muster. It was as if she was speaking not only to Patrick and God, but to all the people in her past life. Then she continued.

Cass said Pleasant finally became very ill and was taken to an army hospital. He still didn't die after a time, so her mother sent some fudge laced heavily with arsenic to the hospital for Pleasant.

"Pleasant still didn't die for some reason, so I had my father pay under-the-table for a quick divorce. Matt and I were ready to leave for Kansas when the word came that Pleasant died. It was apparently a paperwork mix-up, because Pleasant did recover and lived for many years despite our efforts. At the time I didn't regret anything; neither did Mother."

"I left my baby, John, with Pleasant's parents, and didn't try to see him until recently when I needed to be with his family, probably another selfish motive."

Cass let out a long sigh. "So there you have it, Patrick. I hope God will forgive me for being an accomplice to attempted murder and for deserting my baby. I also treated a lot of people badly in my life because of my arrogance and selfishness."

"You have been carrying a heavy burden for a long time, Cass," said Father O'Rourke.

He took her cold hands in his and started his absolution in Latin. He stopped and said, "I'm going to say this in English so you can understand what I am saying. May God give you pardon and peace. You are absolved from all of your sins in the name of the Father, and of the Son, and of the Holy Spirit."

"Thank you, Patrick," Cass whispered. He then administered the last rites for the dying, while Cass started to drift away.

The family doctor was called, and he, Father O'Rourke, and the White family stayed with Cass for the next hour. John, Mary, and her granddaughters gathered around the bed in tears as Cass passed into death with a gentle smile on her face.

THE END

EPILOGUE

LIBERTYVILLE DAILY LEADER
OCTOBER 24, 1920
CASSANDRA BROOKS MARSHAN
DEAD AT AGE 77

Cassandra Brooks Marshan, one of the real pioneer mothers of Libertyville, died Tuesday afternoon at the home of her son, John White, in Indianapolis, at the age of seventy-seven.

The funeral services will be held at the church of St. Brennan's in Indianapolis at 11 AM, Wednesday. Burial will take place at the Riverside graveyard in Libertyville on Friday at 10 AM.

Mrs. Marshan was born in Libertyville on February 22, 1843. She was the daughter of Benjamin and Martha Brooks, who were among the very early settlers in this locality.

Her first husband was Pleasant White of Libertyville, now deceased.

Her second husband, Mathew Johnson, also a native of Libertyville, preceded her in death.

Her third husband, Count Marc Marshan, of Bordeaux, France, is also deceased.

She is survived by her son, his wife, Mary, and three granddaughters, Abby, Jane, and Alice.

****

Cass was right: *"When enough time passes, people forgive or forget."*

Cass' last will and testament provided that her fortune was to be distributed to her three granddaughters, St.Brennan's, and other charities.

The Trouble with Cass

BACKGROUND SOURCES AND REFERENCES

Abraham Lincoln, the Prairie Years and the War Years, Carl Sandburg

Gettysburg National Military Park

Hamilton County East (IN) Public Library-Indiana Room

Hamilton County and the Civil War, J. H. Burgess

Indiana State Archives

Indiana State Museum

U.S. National Home for Disabled Volunteer Soldiers, Dayton, Ohio, and Dayton National Cemetery

National Prisoner of War Museum, Andersonville, Georgia

Stones River National Battlefield Museum, Tennessee

The Civil War, Geoffrey C. Ward

ABOUT THE AUTHOR

C. B. Huesing holds a B.S. degree in Electrical Engineering from Purdue University and an M.S. degree in management and finance from Purdue's Krannert Graduate School of Management.

He was a consultant and a CPA with international accounting firms.

Currently he is working on a sequel to *The Trouble with Cass*. He has written articles on business and sports.

C. B. lives in Indiana with his wife, Nancy. He can be reached at cbhuesing@gmail.com. His web site is www. cbhuesing.com.